THE
LAST
BOY

Also by J.B. Simmons

THE OMEGA TRILOGY
Unbound
Clothed with the Sun
Great White Throne

THE FIVE TOWERS SERIES
The Blue Tower
The Red Tower
The Green Tower
The Yellow Tower
The Black Tower

AND MORE

THE
LAST
BOY

THE GENOME TRILOGY: BOOK ONE

J.B. SIMMONS

Create a world of peace,
Where wars and fightings cease.
Women know what's best:
Put the boys at rest.

The First Mother

1

♂

Wild Bucks

IT'S A BRIGHT SUMMER MORNING when Jude leaves home with his fiddle and a dream to see a real live girl. His big brother Esau leads the way, barreling through the forest like an ox. Dew glistens on fern fronds. Birds sing to their mates. The brothers trek quietly over one ridge, then another, deeper into the wilderness, higher into the hills.

They see no sign of humanity for miles. Jude's legs tire and he misses his family's cabin by the river. Not that he'd dare admit it. He told Ma and Esau he was ready for this.

Esau pauses at a hilltop where moss covers the ground. He glances back at Jude, waiting for him to catch up. "Ya see that buck back there?"

Jude saw only birds and a squirrel. He shakes his head.

"What a rack," Esau says. "Wish I could've taken a shot."

Jude eyes the gun hanging at Esau's back. "Why couldn't you?"

"Ya think the two of us could carry it from here? No use

wastin' the meat. But there will be more. If this ain't Eden there never was one."

Esau bounds off again. Thickets of twigs, thorns, and brambles hardly slow him. Jude stays close until a branch whips back and pokes him in the eye.

He gives Esau more space and wonders at his brother's words. How can any place be Eden without an Eve? The woods seem more like an obstacle than paradise. The pollen makes him sneeze. A bee sting could kill him. Blame allergies, but nature doesn't seem so nice. He prefers the stories he's read about adventures with a cause, maybe even a princess to save. That's why he has to see the Convent. That's where the girls are.

It's been two years since Pa took Esau to see it, from a distance of course. Things didn't go right. Esau came back very different, like someone had sucked up all his laughter and filled him with gravel. Pa didn't come back at all. The Convent captured him, Esau said, but he wouldn't say much more about it.

No wonder Ma was worried this morning. "You're almost a man now," she'd said, as she kissed Jude goodbye. "Nearly as tall as Pa was. He always wanted you to face your fears. But Esau, be very careful. Don't get too close. Keep Jude safe. Stay away from bees. And be back by sundown on Sunday. I'll have dinner ready."

It's late afternoon when the brothers scramble up a rocky outcrop. Sunlight pours over the dense forest like liquid gold. A creek snakes through a valley toward a small lake, clear as a mirror.

Esau points toward the lake. "If I got my timin' right, my friends will meet us there. If we hustle we can make it before dark."

Jude has heard about these *friends*. Esau met them recently while hunting—a duty that fell to him after they lost Pa. Esau said they are three young guys who hiked into the woods from a distant city to get a taste of freedom. They told Esau stories of the "real world" in the Capital, where people have computers and live in tall buildings. Ma has taught them the horrors of that world, of wars and diseases.

Jude pretends like he's not worried. "Let's go," he says.

Another hour of hiking brings them to the lake as the sun sets. The three friends are there, fishing by the shore.

"Hey y'all," Esau hollers to them. "Catch anything?"

They turn with wild grins gleaming through bearded faces. They wear strangely colorful clothing, unlike anything Ma ever made for Esau and Jude. One wears a bright orange coat with a zipper instead of buttons, another an odd red hat with the word "Nike" in bright blue. Jude wonders why guys like these would care about the Greek goddess of victory. And how could they ever hide in the woods with so much color?

"Oh yeah," one of them says. "Big bass in this lake. And Tucker here made a jug of moonshine. Y'all are just in time for supper. Just gotta build a fire."

Esau tells Jude to gather wood, and he does. He makes several trips, listening to the banter about fishing and hunting. They say life's better here than in the Capital, where they work on factory lines, whatever that means. They say they might stay out here forever, even if it is government property.

They light the fire and start to cook. Night falls, enclosing them in darkness. The fish tastes pretty good, salted and fried. When they pass the jug around, Jude sniffs at it and grimaces. Worse than medicine. He passes it on.

"Still just a Mama's boy," Esau taunts. The other guys laugh.

Jude holds his tongue and scoots back a few feet, as if hiding from the group and the firelight. *You don't have to be like Esau*, Ma told him. *He's strong, but you're my virtuoso.* Her words anchor him now. Jude won't let anything get between him and his dream. At least the friends ignore him and don't ask him to play the fiddle. It'd be a shame to perform for animals.

". . . I hear they're from Venus," one of the guys says.

Jude leans in, listening now.

"Venus?" grunts the one named Tucker, with the Nike hat, "Heck, we're only one ridge away from them women. I saw the fence on my way here, in the distance, mind you."

"So what?" Esau says. "I've seen more than the fence. I've seen the Convent. It ain't so special. If ya got the balls to go there."

Jude winces. Esau never talks like this at home. Ma would scrub his tongue with soap.

"Maybe not," another guy says, passing the jug. "As long as you don't let them women see you."

"Ain't that the truth." Tucker takes a swig. "Otherwise you're a goner."

"Why?" Jude asks, too curious to stay quiet.

Tucker eyes him with a devious smile. "Ain't ya heard what happens in Venus?"

"A little," Jude says. "What Esau's told me. The women make the boys do all the work."

"Oh, it's worse than that." Tucker leans forward. His voice lowers. "Folks say it's some kind of experiment. The Capital keeps it all hush hush. Anybody who gets too close never comes back. They'd shave your shaggy hair and make you a slave. And ain't nobody ever made it out of there."

"Then how do you know anything about it?" Jude asks.

"The stories go way back. I once heard an old man say the Capital set it up after a world war, testin' for peace. He said they did other tests with animals, only this one's with boys. Messin' with science and stuff." Tucker grabs his crotch. "Ya know what a gelding is?"

"A horse?" Jude says.

"A horse without balls!" another guy says, and they all laugh.

"So we stallions stay away. To bulls and bucks!" Tucker drinks from the jug, wipes his mouth, and passes it.

"Y'all won't believe the buck I saw today . . ." Esau begins.

Jude's thoughts drift. Is it true, what they said about the Capital and boys? He wonders if that could have happened to Pa. All Esau said, when he came back scraped and bruised and hollow-eyed, was that Pa had been caught. Ma had cried

5

for days. But they hadn't held a funeral.

"...from the fence," Tucker says, drawing Jude's attention again. "I'm tellin' ya, biggest buck I've seen. Just up the east ridge by the lake. But too close to Venus."

The fence . . . just up the east ridge.

The words sink into Jude. He knows where to go. He won't let these fools scare him.

He sleeps for a while, then wakes to the hoot of an owl. It's the middle of the night. Esau and his friends are asleep. Their snores fill the air as Jude slips away in the dark. He leaves his fiddle, safe in its case, because he'll be back soon enough. He just wants a peek. As Pa used to say, you have to see a goal before you can attain it.

It's slow going by moonlight. Jude keeps his breathing and his pace steady. He steels himself against the occasional scurry of leaves. *Deer*, he tells himself. *Maybe even a bear. But they're scared of me, because they don't know me. Same reason I'm scared of girls.*

By dawn's first light he's hiked around the lake and up the east ridge. Along the top runs a high, wire-linked fence with trees cleared on both sides of it. The fence has barbed wire at the top. Signs hang at regular intervals. Each one is faded red and white, with big block letters:

RESTRICTED AREA.

GOVERNMENT PROPERTY.

NO TRESPASSING.

If Esau made it over and back, Jude thinks, *I can, too.*

He climbs it quickly and drops down on the other side,

with only one snag on his pants from the barbed wire. Crouched and wary, he gazes across the valley. The day's first light touches a cluster of white buildings in the distance. It looks like a celestial city hovering above the fog—white and pure and pulling at Jude.

She will be there. A real live girl.

He hikes down into the misty valley and finds a broad river, probably the same one that passes their family's cabin if he judges right. He likes the river in the morning. The water whispers as it gurgles over rocks. Robins chirp in the forest overhead.

This close to the Convent, Jude knows he must move carefully. He walks in the shallows by the river's shore. Water covers his tracks.

He passes a small canoe hidden underneath a willow. Pausing to inspect, he sees *The Odyssey* scrawled on the boat's side. It's the canoe Pa and Esau paddled here, but never brought back. Esau escaped on foot. Jude moves on even more quietly.

A familiar sound stops him.

The moo of a cow. Not far ahead.

He steps silent as a deer up the left side of the riverbank. Through the trees he glimpses a broad grassy field, bordered by a white-picket fence. Up the hill there's a large red barn. Mist hangs low. The morning sun hides behind the veil. The beauty of it makes Jude want to play a pastoral symphony.

But he spies movement by the barn. He hides behind the trunk of a large tree as a group emerges. They wear white robes with their hoods up. He counts twelve figures encircling two cows and another person, in a bright red dress.

It looks like some kind of ceremony.

The one in the red dress turns in his direction. His eyes widen. His heart races.

It's her. A real live girl.

2

♀

Elastrator

HER LADYSHIP NORA, FIRST CLASS, dazzles in her best red dress and yet her story must begin with a plain metal elastrator. Sooner or later every girl in the Convent uses the device. It looks like a large pair of scissors or pliers, like something a dentist would use. Squeeze the grip, expand the thick rubber band, and release it around the round things to be removed.

The twelve mothers stand in white robes watching Nora now. They encircle her and two cows in a green pasture, still wet with dew and shrouded in mist. The Convent is close but out of sight. Beyond the red barn there's the dim outline of forest through the fog.

Nora feels the weight of the world watching her, even if no others are allowed to witness this. Only the mothers. But they are the world to her.

She scans their faces and admires their wise eyes, patient as weathered granite. So stoic, so strong. One day she will become one of them, she feels certain.

This rite of passage is the next step. Every mother has used the elastrator, for it is a necessity. A herd is safe with only one bull and so it must be done.

Nora's thin and delicate fingers, more suited to a violin, squeeze and test the heavy elastrator's grip. Her other hand gently strokes the calf's black and white hide, smooth as velvet. His big innocent eyes show no hint of the threat he'd someday become.

It is the Convent's wisdom to identify danger and remove it before it can grow and spread. This is how they have survived for generations in peace. This is how they will continue to thrive.

The mother cow swings her tail and swats a fly from the calf's moist nose. The pest buzzes away.

Nora and the mother cow exchange a glance. The cow's great glassy stare unsettles Nora, as if the animal suspects the removal of that which would propagate her genes. The mothers say the cow should be here to keep the calf calm. Nora would like a little more space but won't let that, or anything at all, stop her from making the mothers proud.

Will the cow be upset? Nora wonders. *Will she understand?*

Nora laughs inside at her own thoughts, at her nervousness. She can't let the mothers sense her unease. This is a performance like any other.

She takes a deep breath, pulls her dress up, and kneels.

She grips the elastrator harder, stretching the rubber band

again. She steadies her hand as she reaches under the calf.

The cow grunts: *moooo*.

One of the mothers whispers something.

Did I do something wrong? Nora glances back.

The subtle motion causes the elastrator to graze the calf's groin. The calf jerks and kicks.

Nora falls back to dodge the blow. The calf bolts away across the pasture. The mother cow gallops after him. They bound through the field like boulders broken loose from a cliff.

No, no, no, Nora thinks, aghast at her splendid morning spoiled. Dew moistens her backside. Tears well up in her eyes.

"What are you waiting for?" one of the mothers asks. It's Lilith, the first among equals, the lead mother. Her gaze could melt iron. "Finish what you started."

All the white-robed mothers concentrate on her.

Nora feels the heat of their stares like the sun through a magnifying glass. She stands and grits her teeth. *Nature will not be tamed without a fight.* She will not disappoint them. Ceremony is ceremony, and she will see this job done.

She gathers up the red silk hem of her dress with one hand, as the other hand grips the elastrator tight and ready as a sword. Then she runs after the cow and its calf.

She slows as she draws closer. The runaway cows are cornered. They've stopped at the edge of the white-picket fence, surrounded by forest and enclosing a small part of the river shore. The cows stand by the shallows and sip water.

Nora hears a sound, faint as a breath.

11

She glances around and sees the twelve hooded figures following after her like a march of dignified ghosts. It wasn't them. It sounded like it came from the opposite direction. She sees nothing there but the forest.

Focus, she thinks. Maybe she can finish the deed before the mothers even catch up to her. She wants this finished.

She moves steadily toward the calf, the elastrator gripped behind her back. This time she makes no grand display of it. She ignores the mother cow. She slips beside the calf, whispering softly, *shhhh*.

In one smooth and determined motion she kneels, stretches open the tight rubber band, slips it over the dangerous objects hanging from the calf, and releases.

Perfect fit. The calf hardly flinches.

She sighs in relief. The band will now do its work. In a few weeks the danger will be stopped. The herd will be safe.

Nora steps away and an emotion swells in her. Pride and satisfaction at the job done, the obstacle overcome. The mothers will have words for her about letting the calf run away as it did. But she will have her response ready. *This is why we do it when they're young, right? A calf couldn't hurt me but a bull would be a world of trouble. We've tamed another pasture.*

Yes, she is ready to advance.

She gives a parting glance to the cow.

"It's for his good," she says. "And the good of the herd."

A stick snaps. The cow turns and moos.

Nora feels the eyes on her before she sees them.

Peering from behind a tree. It's a person.

It's a . . . *boy*.

3

♂

Campfire

SHE'S A REAL LIVE GIRL. Her red dress blazes as she runs across the grassy field, chasing after two cows. She moves gracefully toward the shallow river. Her hair is short and feathery brown. Her face has perfect lines, smooth skin. Her amber eyes focus on the younger cow.

She stops only twenty feet away.

Jude's heart surges to his throat. He knows he's barely hidden behind a tree, but he can't move.

She kneels and the sun breaks through the mist and glints off a metallic tool in her hand. Slow and steady, she reaches underneath the calf and then does something quick with the tool. Jude can't figure it out, but it sends a chill down his spine. He thought cows were used for only two things: milk and meat.

A stick snaps behind him.

He starts to turn but the girl's face swings toward the sound, toward him.

Their eyes meet.

Jude loses all sense of time and place. Her gaze pulls him forward, more powerful than any magnet. She's too much to be a girl. She must be Venus herself.

Another stick snaps, closer now.

He presses tighter against the tree trunk, clinging to it like a life raft, trying to stay above water, to breathe. He fights the currents sucking him forward, to say hello.

I came here to see, not to be seen. Run, run! It's a faint voice in his mind, and it sounds like Ma, like a voice of reason.

The voice fails. The current is too strong, the girl too powerful.

He steps out from behind the tree. He takes a step forward.

The goddess girl just stares back. She pulls and pulls at him. Her pixie hair, her red dress, her amber eyes . . .

She steps toward him and he steps toward her. He's so close he can see beads of sweat on her divine face. Do goddesses sweat? He burns like Icarus in the sun, too close, too hot to get away.

He holds up his hand, maybe in worship, maybe as hello.

"Who are you?" she calls out.

"Ju—"

A hand suddenly clamps over Jude's mouth. A dark object flashes past his head.

A gun. Pointing at the girl.

"Run, or I'll shoot," growls Esau's voice behind Jude.

The girl's eyes open like a shocked doe before a hunter.

Her face goes white with fear.

No, no! Jude tries to say.

Esau's hand clamps tighter over his mouth so that only a muffled grunt escapes. Jude twists but the girl is already sprinting off and shouting for help.

The gun lowers and Esau drags Jude back, deeper into the trees, away from the girl.

"Let me go!" Jude's shout comes out like a mumble.

Esau finally releases and Jude spins to him in fury.

"Keep quiet or I'll knock ya out," Esau says. "Have ya lost your mind?"

"She wouldn't have hurt me. She was so—" *Beautiful,* he wants to say, but can't.

Esau shakes his head, looking deathly serious. "No. Listen, they're the ones who took Pa. I've been trackin' ya for hours. Wanted to see what you'd do. Now ya dragged us into somethin' didn't ya?"

"I didn't mean to let her see me," Jude says.

"Well now they're gonna come after us. Ma's gonna skin ya, *if* we make it back. Come on, we gotta run. Keep up or I'll shoot ya myself."

Esau races off through the woods, the gun slung over his back. Jude keeps up, like a deer chasing an ox. There's no sound of pursuit. It almost disappoints Jude. He wants to see the girl again.

They follow the same path Jude took into the valley, along the edge of the river. Jude pauses where the canoe is hidden.

"Esau, here's your boat," he says. "Let's take it."

A shadow crosses Esau's face. His dark eyes harden. "Too slow. Come on, faster!"

He charges off again. Jude runs until his heart feels like it will burst. Then he keeps going, propelled by fear and shame.

They finally reach the ridge and the fence at the end of the Convent's territory. Jude pauses at the top. The sun burns bright. The mist has risen. The city shines white in the distance.

"Don't stop there," Esau says, from the other side of the fence.

Jude climbs over and drops down beside his brother.

Esau sighs and wipes the sweat from above his thick eyebrows. "We're safer now."

"But you said they'd come after us," Jude says.

"Not beyond the fence. They don't come out here. But even if they do—" Esau taps his gun— "my friends are armed, too. We'll be safer together."

He and Jude hike back to where they camped the night before. There's no sign of trouble, no hint of Venus. His fiddle is right where he left it. The glassy lake reflects the clear blue afternoon sky. The older guys are all there by the shore. They smell like wet dog.

Esau tells them what happened, how his little brother tried to offer himself up to the Convent. "I had to drag him away from a pretty one in a red dress," he says.

"Whew, that's some balls," one of the friends says, grinning at Jude. "Ya better thank Esau ya get to keep 'em."

"We oughta get movin' and find a new camp," another guy says. "Farther away."

"Nah, ain't nobody takin' us down together," the friend replies, brandishing a rifle. "I figure we set up camp right loud tonight, and if they come we'll snap over 'em like a trap."

Jude grabs Esau's arm and shakes his head. "I don't like it."

"What, ya scared?" Esau says.

"No. Okay, maybe a little. There's only five of us."

"Let 'em come," a guy says. "Out here men get to be men. I'm tired of worryin' about their sick little experiment. It's about time we fight back, protect our huntin' and fishin' grounds. The five of us'll capture 'em, maybe start our own city."

"Let's call it Mars."

"To Mars!" a guy says, holding out a jug.

They toast to it and brag about their plans. Each of them will be armed and ready. They'll build a fire like they suspect nothing, but someone will be on guard. If the women come, they'll make their stand.

Jude listens in disbelief. His own brother, who sounded like the fear of God when he'd seen the girl, now joins the tribe's chorus. Maybe it's the moonshine talking. And the pride of man. Jude decides to pass on both.

"Come on, runt, try a sip," one of them says.

"No, thanks," Jude replies.

"He's still thinkin' about that girl," Esau says.

Jude turns away. Their mocking grows, and so does his

anger.

This time, as dusk falls and the guys ask for a song, Jude agrees to play. He needs to let some energy out before he does something stupid. He pulls out his fiddle and tests the strings, one note at a time. He turns the peg of the E string, making a minute adjustment.

"Come on," a guy grunts. "Quit messin' and play somethin'."

Jude ignores him. He tunes the G string ever so slightly. The note rings soft and true. Then he combines a few notes. His bow glides smooth and draws out the whisper of a chord. The chord expands and pulls Jude with it, into a song.

It's the song that surges out when he thinks of the girl in the red dress. *Salut d'amour*, by Elgar. He loses himself in the notes, in the memory of her amber eyes. The music makes the woods fade, and he's beside her on a mountaintop, in a meadow of wildflowers, where the song is their laughter, their joy.

When he finishes, he looks up and sees the guys' motionless gazes. Their faces range from shock to awe.

"Eh, enough sappy stuff," Esau grunts. "Play us somethin' we can sing to."

There's a moment of silence lingering around the campfire. The guys still stare at him as if seeing a foreign species. One of them says, "Where'd ya learn to do that?"

"Our Ma taught us," Esau says.

"Wait, you can play too?" a guy asks.

"Eh, nothin' like Jude here," Esau says. "He thinks Bach

and Beethoven are his best friends. I always liked huntin' better. Come on now, Jude, play us a fun one."

Jude scowls. Why does his brother have to put on such a show for these guys?

"Please?" Esau says, and the lilt of his voice reminds Jude of Pa. The way he'd talk. Esau looks so much like him.

"All right. Fine." Jude takes a deep breath and plays, *She'll be coming 'round the mountain when she comes.* He plays it hard and fast, letting some of his anger flame out.

The guys sing along raucously around the fire. *Yee-haw!*

Jude secretly hopes the song will come true. Now that he's seen the girl, he'd choose her over these wet dogs.

He offers to take the night's first watch, with a prayer that he'll see her coming 'round the mountain, ridin' six white horses when she comes.

His real live girl in a bright red dress.

4

♀

Hunt

NORA PAUSES TO CATCH HER breath and let the others catch up. The quiet of the dark woods feels heavy. She lifts her night vision goggles and checks her tranquilizer gun. All is in order. She gazes up at the stars through the forest canopy.

Enjoy the hunt, she reminds herself. *Praise Mother God.*

She's dreamed of this for years. It's her new right as a member of First Class, worth all her training, even neutering a calf. Since the morning, she's shed the red dress and the elastrator. Now she wears sleek hunting gear, black as night. She prefers the dress, she admits to herself, but the mothers say surprise is the best way to capture a wild boy.

Leaves rustle nearby.

Nora tenses and pulls the goggles back on. A dim shape approaches. The quick, elegant movements mark her as Valkyrie, one of her sisters, who gives a thumbs up as she leans back against a tree.

Nora chose five women to join her on the hunt. She could have chosen ten or twenty, but she wanted fewer. It's more intimate this way, she thinks. She has only one first capture.

The mothers approved her group readily. Six elite women against a couple wild boys. The Convent had been monitoring the two trespassers the moment they breached the inner territory. When Nora told the mothers, breathless, about the two boys she'd seen, they had calmly told her to select the team to bring them back. "Oh how history's arc has turned," the lead mother Lilith had said, smiling proudly. "Now it takes only six of us to pacify the heirs of war."

They are not just any six, of course. Four of them are veterans with wisps of gray in their hair and jewels around their necks for each of the wild boys they've caught over the years. They've fanned out around Nora now, scanning the trees, protecting. Their jewels glimmer in Nora's goggles. Maybe a dozen total. Valkyrie alone has four captures and four rubies to show for it. She's the best of the best. She could even become the next mother. If tonight goes well, Nora decides she will pick an emerald as her first jewel.

The final member of the hunt comes to Nora's side. It's her best friend, Eve, who is not as fast or experienced as the others, but whose beauty could make her garden-dwelling namesake sick with jealousy. But Nora is not jealous. No, the Convent does not allow jealousy. All are sisters or aunts or mothers.

"Awfully quiet," Eve whispers.

"Was it like this last time?" Nora asks.

"At night, yes," Eve says. "It's better this way, to take the wild ones as they sleep, without any struggle."

"How many do you think there will be?"

"You saw two, so maybe a half dozen. Last time I expected one and there were three. They travel in packs."

The darkness hides Nora's smile. Her eyes flit to the diamond dangling at Eve's neck. She caught a young boy who had been stealing apples from their orchard at the far edge of the Convent's territory. Now he sings in the mothers' choir with the most beautiful soprano.

"How did it feel?" Nora asks. "To capture a real boy?"

The corners of Eve's lips turn up. "It's a great honor. To remove a threat. To serve the mothers."

"You'd be a good mother," Nora says.

"I hope so. You know, the citizen I captured is already like a little sibling to me."

"Because you brought it in?"

Eve nods. "Just in time. It had nearly turned."

"What if my first has turned?" Nora asks.

Eve rolls her eyes like a doting big sister. "That would make the mothers very proud."

Nora turns away to hide her smile. She secretly hopes he will be a man grown. Their territory is so hidden and well-guarded that it's rare to find any wild boys, much less a man. But the woods are thick, and the male species ever roams.

One of the hunters, Min, approaches without a sound. "I found something," she whispers. "Come see."

She leads Nora and Eve to the river nearby. They crouch

by a faint footprint at the edge of water.

"He was careful," Min says. "He stuck to the shallows but made a misstep here."

Nora grins, pleased with her choice of Min. She's the best tracker there is. "Excellent," Nora says. "We'll follow you."

Min leads the six of them along the river. They move like shadows, checking for prints and sniffing for the foul and distinct odor of boy, or even man. Other than a decrepit little canoe, they see no signs of trouble. The trail takes them up a ridge and to the fence that guards their inner territory—where none may enter without consequence.

"Think they crossed here?" Nora asks.

"They must have," Eve says. "Look."

Nora gazes out where Eve points. She sees a thin line of smoke swirling up from the forest. It's as good as a bullseye.

"There's a gate close to here," Valkyrie says.

They follow her to a discreet gate in the fence. Valkyrie lifts her goggles and leans close to the locking device. It scans her retina and opens. Min goes first through the gate. Nora is last, and Valkyrie closes the gate and latch after her.

Nora breathes deeply. It's the first time she's been on the other side. A rare privilege. She takes comfort knowing that the Convent's territory extends many miles beyond this into the wilderness, limiting those who even come close to the fence. She would never leave the outer perimeter, but it's exhilarating to be this far away all the same.

They move silently down a steep slope through the woods, closing in on the source of the smoke. The night air thickens with moisture and warmth. The women move in unison. Frogs croak from the lake ahead. Crickets chirp.

Nora hears a distant crack. One of the prey.

They advance more carefully now. Their night-vision goggles reveal all. Heat sensors show black and blue other than the occasional orange flash of an owl or fox.

"Ohhh."

The faint groan comes deep and guttural from the forest ahead. Only the male species, a wild one, would make a sound like that.

Nora moves forward quick and silent. She hears water flowing like the brisk pour of a tea kettle.

Eve snickers beside her. Her voice is a feather: "He's there."

Nora follows her friend's gaze toward the creature. He is quite a specimen—young but no doubt a man, with ragged hair and a beard like dark wool in the moonlight. His hands hold . . .

"Oh my," Nora whispers.

Liquid streams yellow as a comet through her goggles.

Eve puts her hand on Nora's shoulder. "Quick, take the shot."

Nora draws her tranquilizer gun. She takes a deep breath, trying to steady her racing heart. She glances at the other women beside her. Valkyrie nods. They are ready. Nora focuses on the man, the threat. She aims at his neck, below the beard. And for the good of the Convent, she fires.

The dart hits right where she aimed. The man staggers,

then goes down like a falling tree. He lands with a loud thud.

Others stir closer to the fire. Nora scans the camp and sees three of them, moving quickly. They're on their feet in a moment.

"Hey!" one of them shouts. "Attack!"

"Masks," Valkyrie orders. "Gas."

Valkyrie tosses a canister toward the fire pit, gas streaming as orange smoke. Nora and the others throw their own canisters. It's enough gas to put a village to sleep.

The males go down. The women stalk forward to inspect the camp, with dart guns raised. They are young men. Each one is bearded, though unwrinkled. None look older than twenty. Their camp smells of fire, fish, and alcohol.

Through her thrill of capture, something nags at Nora. Something missing.

The boy, she thinks. The one she saw in the morning. He had shaggy dark curls and no beard. He was younger. He was different.

She studies the camp more closely. Her heat sensor detects a soft glow of warmth on the ground, further from the fire than the others, as if someone had laid in the spot not long ago. She raises her mask to inspect it. It's more neatly arranged than the others.

"Well done!" Eve says, coming to Nora's side and clasping her shoulder. "We've got them all. The mothers be delighted. Which one will you want to tame?"

Nora points to the empty spot on the ground. "The one that got away."

5

♂

Escape

THE SMOOTH BLACK SURFACE of the lake glitters with stars. Jude has been on watch for a while. He sat still. He paced to stay awake. Now he stands at the water's edge, gazing out and thinking about the girl. He wears his fiddle strapped to his back. He wants to play but knows he shouldn't risk a single note in the tranquil night. He imagines the song. It rises and falls as he wonders, *what's her name?*

A faint grunt makes him turn. It's Esau, with his back to Jude, letting out some of the moonshine.

Jude starts to laugh but it freezes in his throat when Esau suddenly staggers. His brother goes rigid and collapses, with a hand to his throat. The night erupts in a sudden flurry of movement.

Dark figures charging.

The guys stirring.

Metallic clinks on the ground.

Jude reacts instantly, just as Ma taught him. He drops flat

to the shore and slips into the icy water, smooth as a snake. No time to drop the fiddle. No splash. No gasp at the cold.

He is shoulder deep before he risks another glance back. It's a nightmare come to life. Smoke in the moonlight. Shadowy figures race through the camp. They are nearly invisible until a flashlight beams through the smoke. Two of them stand by the place where he slept, inspecting it. They wear all black, with strange masks over their faces and small guns in their hands. They must be from the Convent. They must have tracked them through the forest. From what the guys said, they won't be men much longer. Esau was no saint but he doesn't deserve this.

Gripped by guilt but helpless to stop it alone, Jude flees. He swims as fast and as silent as he can, mostly below the surface and coming up for only a few quick breaths. His fiddle might be ruined but he has no choice. A splash could mean the end.

They see in the night, Ma once said. *They detect heat.*

He'd thought it was just a story she told to keep him close to their cabin. He was wrong. He has to get home. Ma will know what to do.

He rounds a bend in the lake so that the ambushers are out of sight. He rises at the edge of a cove and glides silently into the trees, dripping water as he goes. Danger presses him on, heart pounding, through the thick forest and up a steep hillside.

The slope rises to a crest. He glimpses the wire fence a stone's throw away. He'll go no closer, but he moves parallel to it, along the ridge. It should lead to the river, which he can follow to home. He keeps up his pace. He knows the Convent might pursue him, and the fence won't stop them.

He pauses before a clearing to catch his breath. He hears a dull whir. He looks up to the canopy of the forest, where the first light of gray dawn touches the sky. The sound takes form as a blur hovering overhead.

They have drones, Ma said. *Like the ones used in the old wars.*

Jude's stomach sinks. They have guns and a flying machine. He has no chance, but he has to try. For Ma. She'd never recover if she lost both her boys.

He hunkers as low as he can under a thick bush. The drone zigs and zags over the trees, pausing at times in midair like a hummingbird, only to dart forward again. It swoops over Jude and away toward the lake.

He wipes sweat from his forehead and moves forward again. The morning comes to life with the sounds of birds and squirrels. Their happy banter nearly hides the sudden snap of a twig. A shiver runs down Jude's spine. He glances back and sees nothing. Still, he feels sure it was no creature of the forest.

He takes off sprinting. The ridge levels out on a bald expanse of stone hanging over the river. He's made it, but he'll be exposed. Only a few twisted pines could provide cover, breaking through cracks in the rock. There's no more sound of a drone. No rustling or broken twigs.

He stays low as he rushes out onto the rocky ledge. He's twenty paces from a cliff, close enough to hear the gurgling water below, when something hard thuds into him.

He stops in shock and crouches behind a pine. Reaching back, he plucks off a metal dart. It hit his fiddle, not his skin.

A figure emerges out of the woods.

It's her, the goddess.

Her mask is off. Even without the red dress, wearing black head-to-toe, Jude recognizes her face, her intense amber eyes.

Jude backs away but knows he doesn't have much room. He clutches the fiddle to his chest like a shield.

She raises a hand innocently, as if in peace. "Who are you?"

Her siren's voice pulls at Jude.

His thoughts flicker to Ma, reading a story to him. Odysseus made his sailors tie him to the mast. They stuffed beeswax into their ears. Only then could he hear the sirens. Jude has no mast and no wax. He's doomed.

When sirens call, Ma said. *You run, Jude. Run home.*

He forces himself to keep moving, backing one step at a time as the girl approaches. Their gazes are locked, drawing together like magnets.

"Careful!" she says.

Jude's foot comes to the edge. He glances down. A twenty-foot drop to the river. *Is it deep enough?*

"I won't hurt you." The girl takes another step. She's only ten paces away. A real live girl.

Jude can see beads of sweat on her perfect brow, beneath her perfect pixie hair. "What's your name?" he manages.

"Nora. And you?"

"Jude."

The faintest of grins touches her lips. "I saw you in the morning, by the pasture. I've been trying to find you. I just want to talk."

I'd like that, Jude thinks, but behind the girl two dark figures advance from the woods onto the bare stone expanse.

The girl follows his gaze and holds up her hand. "No, wait!" she calls out to the others.

But Jude has snapped out of his trance.

The other two are no girls. They are women, stern and intense. He thinks again of Odysseus, between Scylla and Charybdis. He has to make it home. Gazing down at the water, he eyes a calm and deep spot. He opts for the whirlpool over the monster. With a final, longing glance at Nora, he turns away and leaps off the cliff.

6

♀

Triumph

MORNING IS RADIANT AT THE CONVENT. Golden light shines on the white buildings and streets, like the glow of heaven. Bells ring to mark the start of day, then they ring again. *Ding, dong, ding.* Three chimes. It means a celebration, a welcoming for the victorious. The community comes to the white pillars that mark the city entrance. They need no wall or gate. They live in peace. Hundreds of them gather, clad in white, excitement in their eyes. It has been over a year since the last capture.

Nora strides from the fields toward the Convent and the crowd. This should be her proudest moment. Her inaugural hunt has succeeded. They expected two wild boys, and she has brought back four young men. And so she smiles, as she should, but the smile masks disappointment. Her mind fixates on the boy she lost.

He was within her grasp. Her shot was blocked, but she had him engaged, talking. She could read him. He would not have leapt off the cliff if not for Valkyrie and Min showing up and scaring him. He was wild, yes, but something else stirred in him. It was almost . . . sensitive. His dark green eyes had such energy, such depth . . .

Enough of that, she tells herself. He was a threat, and she could have tamed him. But now he's probably dead. They didn't see his body rise in the river. What a waste.

Keep smiling, Nora. Smile.

She wears a triumphant face as she leads the group toward the entrance. Her five companions follow in wedge formation, surrounding the four captives. Their shaggy heads are up, eyes ogling in amazement at their first sight of the Convent. Nora imagines their wonder at the orderly streets of brick, at the clean white buildings, at the peaceful crowd. Perfect rows of rosebushes line the walkways. The air is fragrant with their sweet perfume. The Convent offers everything that these wild boys could never have on their own.

Nora brings her group to a halt inside the pillared entrance. The twelve white-robed mothers approach from the Great Hall on the hill above. They glide forward like a flying V of swans, elegant and proud. As they come to a stop before Nora's entourage, the onlookers huddle closer. Hundreds of eager faces gather to see a wild boy and what the mothers will do.

"One from First Class comes," a mother says.

"She comes to give her bounty," the other mothers chant back. In unison, the mothers pull back their hoods.

Nora curtsies before them. She steps to the side, allowing the mothers to view her captives. "We bring four wild males," she says.

Her statement needs no inquiry. The captives, even with their mouths clamped shut, provide the answers. Ragged hair, unkempt beards, shabby clothes, smudged faces. If not for the sedatives, they'd probably be snarling and shouting, too.

"Well done. Well done indeed." Lilith, the lead mother, steps forward with the grace of a queen in her white robe. Only the other mothers may call her by name. Her pepper-gray hair is shaved close. Her intense blue eyes meet Nora's. "They look most wild. And yet you bear no wound. Was there no fight?"

"We came upon them at night," Nora says. "We tranquilized them before any struggle."

"This is good. It is our way, always, to seek peace." Lilith clasps her shoulder. "You have proven your merit as First Class."

Nora bows her head. "Thank you, mother."

"And we thank you." Lilith turns to the crowd and spreads her arms wide, as if in invitation. "How do we reward such loyalty?"

"With life!" the crowd answers.

"With life," Lilith replies. "We shall see which of these wild ones may bring new life to the Convent. They will be tested. Let's have a first look."

Lilith moves toward the captives. While her plain robe speaks of modesty, her jewels show her power. Twelve precious stones glimmer in the morning light at her fingers and ears and neck. The centerpiece, hanging from her necklace, is a ruby the size of a strawberry. It belongs only to the lead mother, first among equals.

The males, sedated as they are, look at the woman and her jewels in wonder. Three of them step back as she approaches.

"Come now," she says. "I do not bite."

The crowd laughs with nervous energy, their gazes riveted.

Lilith faces the male who did not step back. Nora recognizes him as the one she first saw and took down. The mother grips his chin in her wiry hand and inspects him like a piece of fruit in a produce stand.

"You have spirit," she says. "What's your name?"

His voice comes out faint but sure: "Esau."

"You will play for us, Esau. And we'll see if you have what it takes."

"Play what?" he asks.

"Why, music of course. We create beauty here. You will see." Lilith releases him and moves to the next one. He wears a hat with the word "Nike" on it. When she reaches for his chin, he swats her hand away.

"Hm, trouble. The vile T. This one is full of it." Lilith turns to the crowd. She calls out: "What do we do with trouble?"

"Remove it!" the crowd answers.

"Yes, yes. Some have no hope of taming." She faces the young man again. "Kneel."

He stays on his feet.

"This will be your last chance," Lilith says. "Kneel."

He looks to the others as if hoping for help. They've stepped away from him. He's alone. He meets Lilith's gaze. Warily, like a cornered fox, he starts to kneel. As he lowers he hurls his hat high into the air. The crowd's eyes follow the hat. The male suddenly sprints away.

"Stop the citizen," Lilith says.

He has made it only twenty feet when five darts pluck into his back. He staggers and falls.

Lilith motions dismissively. "Pacify it."

Valkyrie and Min rush forward and haul his limp body away.

Lilith proceeds to the next young man as if nothing has happened. She inspects him. He does not resist.

It is the same with the fourth captive.

When the inspection is complete, Lilith turns to Nora again. "Three potential seeds, and one servant already. Well done indeed."

Nora's heart sings. "Thank you, mother."

Lilith flashes a rare smile, then turns to face the crowd. "All of you, back to your tasks," she orders. "Firsts, you have earned a day of rest. Bathe and sleep. Soon you will need to test these three who remain. Perhaps you will find one who is suitable for harvest, for the seed of new life in the Convent."

7

♂

Home

JUDE GAZES DOWN INTO THE valley and lets out a homesick sigh. After trekking for hours, he's made it back alone and empty-handed. The cabin in the valley isn't much to look at, not after the city or the girl. Smoke drifts up from the little chimney. The faded barnwood walls and red tin roof seem more suited for housing chickens than humans. But he knows better. As he limps forward he recognizes the Ma's tender touches. Freshly washed clothes hang on a line by the garden. Lavender blooms along the steps of the stone path.

Jude plucks a small purple flower as he passes. The fragrance helps him forget for a moment the leap into the river, the stone that gashed open his knee, and the hiding under the frigid water. But the smell, soft and lovely, only sharpens his memory of the real live girl who caused it all: Nora.

I've been trying to find you, she said.

And maybe we'll find each other again, he thinks.

He decides not to tell Ma about that. He reaches the front door and raises his hand to knock. Before he touches the wood, a shotgun cocks inside.

"Who is it?" Ma calls out.

"It's me. Jude."

His dog Locke barks with excitement. The door doesn't open. He feels like Odysseus returning home.

"Were you followed?" she asks.

Jude smiles as he remembers the code words. "Foxes have holes, but I have nowhere to lay my head."

The lock unbolts and the door swings open. Ma's arms are around him and Locke is licking his ankles and he feels safe for the first time since Esau brought him to the camp by the lake.

Ma picks over him like a chimp grooming an infant. "What took you so long?" Starting with his mop of tangled hair, her hands quickly poke and prod until they find the bloody spot on his knee. "Oh, you're hurt. And you're filthy, skin and bones. Have you eaten a single thing? You didn't get close to any bees, did you? Wait, where's Esau? Where's your fiddle? What happened?"

Jude thinks again of the girl and flushes but doesn't stop Ma. He's seen her like this when Esau used to return from nights away—a complete inspection, a barrage of questions, and no time for answers. She's plucked a dozen ticks from scalps over the years. And once she found on Esau a candy wrapper laced with a tracker. He never picked up candy again.

Ma steps back and seems satisfied that Jude is, in fact, her son and that he is alive and sanitary enough to enter the cabin. She ushers him to the little table for breakfast. There's only one room downstairs. The kitchen on one side, the sitting area on the other. Books and musical instruments line the walls. A small fire crackles in the stone hearth.

Jude sits down to a plate of bacon and eggs. Even though he's starving, he can't take a bite before he tells her.

"Ma, they got Esau."

She freezes, then sits across from him. "How?"

Jude tells her what happened in careful detail. The camp of guys, the attack by night, and his escape. He doesn't say a word about the girl. Ma seems to sense he's leaving something out but doesn't pry. She seems as serene as a mountain lake, which happens whenever she's disturbed.

Jude sips his milk and wipes his mouth with his sleeve and Ma doesn't even tell him to use a napkin. This is very bad.

"They will come here soon," she says.

"Why? They've never caused us trouble."

"Because they didn't know about you and Esau. Now they have Esau. They'll ask him questions."

"He won't answer them. Not Esau. Pa didn't, did he?"

Ma looks at Jude long and hard until she sighs and smiles. "I've always loved your spirit. So innocent. Pa used to be like that." She gazes out the window like she sees something far off in the distance. "Remember that time you planted our corn rows crooked?"

Jude remembers well. Pa had been out planting in the spring. He'd had their two mules pulling hard. Esau and Jude followed after them, each to a row, dropping corn kernels into the rich, turned-over soil. While he worked, Jude hummed a song he'd been practicing on the fiddle, not paying enough attention. A month later, as the corn grew, they discovered that the rows didn't follow a straight line.

"I'll never forget," Jude says.

"What did Pa say?"

Jude can still picture Pa's wide grin across the dinner table. "He said there was a message in the corn for me, written in treble clef."

"A message from Vivaldi," Ma adds.

"Yes," Jude says with a laugh. "The message was to play my music, not plant it."

Ma puts her hand over Jude's. There's a shadow over her eyes. "Pa grew up free. He wanted the same for you."

Jude wonders how much she knows that she hasn't told him. "Ma, Esau's friends said they were from the Capital. What kind of place is it?"

"It's a city. A dangerous and powerful city. They established the Convent long ago, and they guard it still. Those boys Esau met should never have entered this territory."

"You mean we're on the Convent's land?" Jude asks.

She nods. "Only the outer perimeter. Not too close."

"How far is the Capital?"

"Much farther away. It would take many days, maybe weeks to get there."

Jude thinks of the untouched wilderness around them, as

far as he can see. "Why do we live *here*, Ma?"

"I've told you before. Pa and I found a place where we could be free, where we could raise you and your brother with truth and love, where we could raise you to be men."

"I know, but they took Pa and Esau."

"They haven't taken you." Her eyes are moist as she gently touches his cheek. "Remember, one good man can save the world."

That's what they've taught Jude, but he couldn't even save his brother. "How is that possible?"

"You will see," she says. "For everything there is a season."

Jude has heard her say that a thousand times. "Like a time for war, and a time for peace?"

"Yes, and a time to keep, and a time to cast away."

"You think we have to leave?"

"You'll be a man soon." She rises from the table and returns with a small leather bag. "Pa wanted you to have this."

She unzips the bag. Jude gazes at the treasure inside. There's a brass-handled shaving razor, a foaming brush, and a few other grooming things. Pa used it every morning.

"Why are you giving me this?" Jude asks.

"Because it's time," she says. "More eggs?"

He says yes and feels fear taking root down to his toes. *It's time. A time to cast away. Pa would've wanted you to have this.* The truth hits him harder than it could in the wild: Esau's gone, Pa's gone, and Jude is all Ma has left.

8

♀

Citizen

NORA PACES IN THE HALLWAY outside the door. The thick red carpet and curtains muffle the voices inside the room. Her heart pounds against her violin, clutched tight under her arm. The instrument's familiar curve of wood and smell of rosin should ease her nerves. She's the one in control. She captured this young man behind the door. She snuck up on him in the forest. He was like an animal, grunting and . . .

She blushes at the memory. Good thing it was night.

Four citizens pass on their way out to work in the fields. They sing a joyous morning song, their high voices in unison, their light brown clothes clean before a good day of work. They have their duty and she has hers.

She twirls the violin bow as she waits. It's been a big week, that's all. First the calf running away from the elastrator, then the capture, and now her first testing. Plenty of opportunities to live into her destiny as First Class. And someday, maybe, to join the mothers.

There's nothing to worry about, she assures herself. He will be a citizen like all the others. But could he be a sire?

The door swings open and one of the mothers emerges. She closes the door before Nora can even glimpse the prospect.

"All's ready," the mother says. Her name is Krystal, and many consider her the second most important mother. Her long graying blonde hair is pulled back tight as if extending her wise and solemn expression. She looks incapable of surprise. "Are *you* ready?"

Nora's left hand tightens around the neck of the violin. All she has to do is play. "Yes, mother."

"The citizen is unbound but the source of danger is gone."

Nora's breath catches in her throat. "It's gone?"

"Yes, we deemed it unfit to be a sire."

"Why?"

"Not enough genetic variety," Krystal says. "Also, too aggressive and untameable. Sometimes the older ones cannot be redeemed."

Nora knows better than to question the mysteries that only the mothers can know. Genetic testing. Seed harvesting. Pairing and birthing. She replies, "I see."

"Be careful in there. It will take a while for its T to fall."

Nora shudders at the mention of the hormone—what they call testosterone, trouble, or simply T. They've done so much to guard themselves against it, but still she can't help feeling a little disappointment. Her first capture has gone from *he* to *it* before she could even test the potential.

"Do not worry," the mother says. "The guards will be close if you need help. Our new citizen says it knows how to play. Maybe it will serve the First Class rather than work the fields. We will let you be the judge of that."

"Thank you," Nora says.

The mother turns with a satisfied smile and glides away down the hall, her white robe like a splash of foam rising from the long river of red carpet.

Nora faces the door and takes a deep breath. She enters like a princess come to inspect her new gelding.

The citizen sits in the center of the room on an ornate wooden chair. It reclines with legs extended and ankles crossed. It eyes Nora in a way wholly unsuited to a citizen. Like she's an equal. Or worse, like she's prey.

"What's your name?" she asks.

"Esau." It comes out like a challenge.

"What did the mother call you?"

"That old lady in the robe?"

Its tone strikes her like a slap across the face.

Dignity, Nora. You're in control. "Yes."

"She called me E11. Makes me wonder where the first ten E's are. I figure y'all locked 'em up somewhere."

"I'm here to see how you play."

"I heard." It glances at the violin clutched by Nora's chest. Its eyes linger there. "Why do y'all care so much about music?"

Nora can't resist a smile. "What would you care about if

there were no war or struggle?"

"Sounds boring. Maybe food."

"Yes, we eat well. But we battle over beauty, and music is our favorite sword. It spills joy rather than blood. How did you learn?"

"Ma taught me. Made us practice every day. Bet ya can't keep up."

"Well then." Nora raises her violin. "Let's find out."

Nora warms up with a few scales. No vibrato. A clear and pure sound, simple and profound.

The citizen lifts the violin that has been left for it. Its large hands have a softer touch than Nora expects.

"Want to try following me?" Nora asks.

"I'll lead."

"Fine, play whatever you like."

E11 crams the violin into the nook of its muscled neck. Veins bulge behind the beautiful curve of amber wood. Its grip is far too tight. This should be the delicate moment, the quiet before the dawn of sound. Nora cringes at the brusque handling and waits for the scratchy cacophony of a novice.

Then the citizen breathes in deep through its nose, eyes on the strings. Its sinewy arms spring into motion like the release of a rubber band pulled taut.

The sound comes fast and violent. Notes flurry and trill.

Nora steps back. It's so loud. Not beautiful. Not delicate. But amazing in its own way.

The citizen does not slow or doubt. It plays like someone running for its life. The quick melody draws Nora in and up and she loses her sense of place and time. There is only the rush of trills, jumping octaves, masterful.

The final note explodes with no less force than the first.

Then, silence.

E11 glares at Nora as the memory of sound reverberates in the small room. It wipes at the sheen of sweat across its broad forehead.

She steadies her breathing, releasing the exhilaration of the song. "What do you call that?"

"The Devil's Trill by Tartini. Didn't care to play along?"

"I've never heard it. It was . . . fast. Few play at that tempo here."

"Eh, my little brother can do it with his eyes closed."

Little brother, Nora thinks. *He must be the one I saw. The one who got away.* "I'd like to meet him."

"Want to tame him, too? Ma won't allow it."

Nora suppresses a grin. This is helpful information. They will find this dangerous home and the missing boy.

"We do not tame," she says. "We only give peace. You will be free here. You are a citizen now."

"Some freedom if you won't let me leave."

"It's for your own good. There's no better place than the Convent."

"My place is in the wild, as you people call it."

"You will learn. No one's place is chaos. Humans are designed for order. Even your song, this Devil's Trill, arises from a careful order, even if it sounded at times of chaos. Surely you know that."

"It was the chaos you liked."

She shakes her head. "No, you are mistaken."

"I saw the way you watched me play."

"Well, it *was* moving. But it was the order and the way you shared it. The Convent is the perfect place to share beauty. The perfect audience."

"I'm my own audience."

"Let's continue. You will see. You will learn the truth."

It crosses its arms, knuckles white around the violin neck gripped in its hand.

Nora smiles gently. This is progress. E11 expects force, like anyone would from the wild. It has much to learn of the Convent's ways. Nothing is ever forced, once T is removed.

She raises her violin in an elegant sweep, her smile unfaltering. Deep breath. She copies his notes in a slower tempo. The sound jumbles slightly. She tries again, and again.

"G after A, right?"

The citizen's hard stare softens. It grunts and nods, arms still crossed.

This time Nora gets most of the first line. She moves to the second. "Is it an E here?"

"Yes, but . . ."

"What?"

It sighs and lifts its violin. The bowing is rigid but moving, bending. Iron must melt before it can be molded. E11 will be malleable. No one can resist the Convent's sweet song.

It plays the next three notes. Nora copies.

"Then what?" she asks. "I'm sorry, you were moving so fast."

It blinks as if surprised at her admission. "Yeah, it's fast."

As they play on, Nora glories in the little drops that melt from E11's hard facade. The mothers in their infinite wisdom know this truth. It's the slow and steady river of gentleness that erodes mountains. With E11's body now working for peace inside, removing the source of anger and hostility that defines its sad caste, and with Nora patiently working her magic, this citizen will become as faithful as any other. Yes, E11 will become a fine citizen.

And its little brother will be next. She will find him.

9

♂

Burning

A WHOLE ROASTED CHICKEN, a feast, steams on the small table. Jude slept until midday and now he sits across from Ma. She prays and they eat. Locke sleeps on the floor at their feet. It's too quiet. Half of their family is gone, the louder half.

Ma breaks the silence. "There's a storm coming."

"How do you know?" Jude asks.

"I feel it in my bones. But it will pass." The crow's feet at Ma's eyes crease in tension, despite her attempt to smile. "Better eat up. Have another drumstick?"

Jude takes another drumstick. He asks a few questions about Pa and the Convent, but Ma clams up.

"Let's not worry about that now," she says. "Some things are better not to know. What are you going to read tonight?"

They talk about their books, full of old histories and tales. That's the one thing they can always talk about. Their little library holds a world of conversation.

As Jude gnaws meat from a bone, he's reminded of his brother and a story he's heard a hundred times. It's about twin brothers, and the younger one stole the birthright.

"Ma, why'd you and Pa choose the name Esau?"

"We've told you. It's a strong name, especially out here in the wilderness."

"I know. But does that make me Jacob?"

She puts her fork down slowly, green peas falling back to her plate. "No. Your name is Jude. You weren't even a twinkle in my eye when we had Esau."

"Then he turned out strong, a hunter. And I . . ."

"You became what your name means."

"Praised. Maybe by you."

"Oh you'll find more praise than that. Mark my words."

"Praised like Jacob, or his son Judah? Not so great . . ."

"Their stories show you can be chosen to do something important even when you don't deserve it. But I think you will deserve it. You have unique talent."

"What, with music?" Jude shakes his head. "I don't even have a fiddle anymore."

"You can use Pa's. Trust me, you'll find a way to shine."

Jude says thanks but feels unsatisfied. His mother's praise is like another drop of water in a lake she's already filled up.

When they finish dinner, Jude chooses a worn book about ancient Greek history. It seems better than his life—full of wars and gods, heroes and villains. Ma busies herself with dishes, humming Esau's favorite song, the Devil's Trill.

Jude's eyelids have begun to droop when Locke growls at

his side. He pets his old dog and feels hair bristling at the neck. The dog stalks toward the door and barks.

Ma's hand touches Jude's shoulder. Her face is drawn tight as rawhide. "Come," she whispers. "Down to the cellar, take the tunnel. Stay hidden until the storm passes."

Locke still crouches at the door, snarling.

Ma and Jude move fast and silent. Together they slide away the rug covering the cellar door and drop down. Once inside, they open a large chest at the back wall and unlock the hidden panel at the bottom. A little square hole of darkness yawns up at them.

Ma hands him a backpack. "Be good and strong and courageous, okay?"

"When will I see you again?"

She clasps his peach-fuzz cheeks in her weathered hands. Her blue eyes glisten like a glacier. "I love you. Now get going."

He drops into the hole and sees Ma gazing down as she closes the hidden door. The trunk shuts with the loud creak of old wood. Locke's vicious barks should hide the sound.

Jude crawls through the narrow passage. It smells like a catacomb. He feels along the walls in the pitch-black.

A sharp whelp of pain makes him freeze.

There's a faint thump above.

"Welcome, Krystal." Ma's voice, even muffled through the cellar floor, sounds steady as rain. "It's awfully late to come all the way out here. Especially with a storm brewing."

"Oh, we both know why I'm here," a woman replies. Her

voice sounds like a steel drum.

"I expected you next week, but nice to see you all the same. Tea?"

"Yes, please. With mint if you don't mind."

"Of course."

The floor creaks overhead. Jude knows he should go but he dares not abandon Ma. He creeps back and cracks open the trunk. He sits still as a rock, peering out of the trunk's lid to the floor above. His eyes have adjusted a bit. Through a crack in the floorboards he spots a black boot with drops of red on it.

"You know," says the woman. "You really ought to have your dogs spayed. We never mean any harm, of course, but aggression cannot be tolerated."

"Locke was a good dog."

"What a pity. Next time you have a good male pup send him our way. He might even become a sire. We can't sire any males who've grown wild out here, you know."

"Yes. I know."

There's a long quiet, tense as the seconds between lightning and thunder.

The tea kettle whistles.

"That was fast. Water must have been warm already."

"I usually have a cup of chamomile before bed."

The woman lets out a sharp laugh. "Do you think I toy with you? So sorry. We go way back, friend. Where is he?"

"You already have him," Ma says.

"J2, yes. And your son?"

"He's gone now. I thought you had him, too."

"Now that you mention it, yes, we do. And he said he has a little brother. Need I ask why a second fork sits on the table?"

"I keep it there," Ma says. "In case he comes back. It gets mighty lonely out here. Since you took my husband."

"Don't use that word with me. Now come along."

"I can't leave."

"Don't you want to see your son?"

Ma lets out a long sigh. "I'll think it over as we finish the tea."

"Should I search the place as you sip?"

"No need," Ma says.

"I doubt that. Do not try anything foolish. As I'm sure you know, I did not come alone. The place is surrounded."

"I see." Ma's voice is calm, too calm.

"I'll give you a couple minutes to gather your things. Sorry, friend, there won't be any coming back. The mothers have decided you cannot remain here. I almost wish we'd never allowed it in the first place."

"Well, then. Time to cast away." Ma rises and the floor creaks as she moves overhead.

Jude uses the cover of sound to close the trunk and crawl away through the tunnel. He shuffles fast on his hands and knees. He can't hear them talking now. But he heard enough. They have Esau. They know about him. They could find him if they search. He moves as quietly as he can in the darkness.

Bam.

The sudden sound stops him.

Even through the floor and the ground and the tunnel, the blast of the shotgun is unmistakable.

No, God no.

There's a murmur of more noises, muffled by the earth. It sounds like a struggle, but no more gunshots.

Jude forces himself to press on. He can't go back. He tells himself they wouldn't hurt Ma. The woman named Krystal called her friend. The woman with blood on her boot.

Be strong and courageous, Ma said. *Time to cast away.*

He keeps going. He passes the safe room. There's no more safety here. He pays no mind to the tears falling down his cheeks.

The tunnel ends in a small opening at the edge of the river. The sky is darker. The air smells of smoke. He crawls up the riverbank and sees his family's cabin, his only home, burning.

10

♀

Papilla

NORA CRACKS THE EGG AND lets the yolk run yellow on the white plate. She dabs her finger and licks the warm viscousness. The egg must have been laid just this morning. It tastes like life, like the beginning of another brilliant day in the Convent.

She focuses on her morning prayers as she eats.

In the beginning Mother God created the heavens and the earth and all that is in it.

She knows the creed by heart. She doesn't remember a day when she hasn't said it. Nor does anyone else in the Convent. From Mother God to the first mother Eve to the lead mother Lilith, all descend from the goodness of woman and all serve to tame the evils of man. She understands it better now, having seen the change in E11. He is softening already. He will be a good citizen.

Today she will practice with him again. She wants to know more about how he learned. His way of playing is both familiar and strange, like a wild offshoot from her same vine.

She finishes the first egg and washes it down with fresh milk. She has just tapped the delicate shell of the second egg when her door opens.

Selene, one of the mothers, stands in the doorway.

Nora rises quickly and bows, trying to mask her surprise.

"Good morning, child."

"Good morning, mother." Nora straightens her sleeping garments. She has not even brushed her hair yet.

Selene's hands are clasped tightly. Her round face looks weary beneath a bob of graying brown hair. She glances at Nora's plate, where the cracked egg still wobbles. "You may finish, if you'd like."

"Thank you. But please, how can I serve?"

"This will be an important day for you."

"Every day is important in the Convent."

"Well said, and this one especially so." Selene looks down at her hands. "One of the mothers passed away last night."

Nora takes a step back. "Mother God, bless her soul."

"Yes. Krystal went peacefully in her sleep."

Krystal. Nora saw her just days ago. She looked perfectly well, with her long gray-blonde hair and wise eyes. Many expected her to be the next lead mother. "This is a tragic loss."

"Death is always a loss for us, but a blessing for the departed. It can also bring opportunity."

"What do you mean?" Nora asks.

"We will need a new mother. There will be a competition tonight. Lilith sent me to talk with you about that."

Me? So soon? A competition? Who will it be? Nora resists the urge to blurt out her questions, to leap, to sing, with excitement and fear of what this could mean.

"I have just become First Class," she says.

"And made your first capture. Your rise is impressive. Speaking of that . . ." The mother reaches into a fold of her white robe and holds out a small velvet box. "Lilith chose this for you. Go ahead. Open it."

Nora takes the box and lifts the lid. She lets out a gasp. Inside is a brilliant emerald. She lifts it by the thin silver chain in the box, eyes lost in its many facets.

"I'll help you try it on," Selene says, moving behind her and clasping the chain. She points over Nora's shoulder to the mirror. "Have a look."

Nora soars as she sees the reflection. It's just what she dreamed of. "How did you know I wanted this?"

"Lilith spoke with Eve." Selene moves around to face Nora again. "The color suits you well."

"It's amazing. I . . . where do we get such jewels?"

"Ah," Selene says. "You may learn someday, if you keep up this pace. Only a few mothers know that."

"Thank you. I live only to serve the Convent."

Selene nods toward Nora's small desk and the plate there. "Please, finish eating and dress. I would like to walk while we talk. I will wait outside until you are ready."

"Thank you, mother. I will be quick."

"You always are." The mother turns with a sweep of white robe and closes the door behind her.

Nora falls back to sit on her bed, trying to collect herself. A mother has never visited her room before, and to come unannounced and to tell her a mother died and to talk about becoming a mother and to give her an emerald.

Well, it is a great honor. That's what it is.

The Convent and the mothers have prepared her for this. She will not shy away. And she must not keep Selene waiting.

She eats the second egg quickly. She goes to her wardrobe, where two new dresses hang—the gifts given to the First Class. She brushes her hair as she decides on the green dress, matching the jewel and cut to the knees, good for walking. She slips it on, along with her black boots. She washes down her food with a sip of milk. With a final glance to ensure all in her room is in order, as it always is, she leaves.

Selene waits solemnly in the hall. "You look nice, child."

"Thank you, mother."

"Come, I would like to show you something." Selene strides down the hall. They pass a few young women, still apprentices, the level below First Class, whose eyes widen when they see Selene and who give Nora a double take. She doesn't normally dress like this, and a mother almost never visits the dorms. But now Nora is First Class, head held high, a leader in the making.

Outside, the Convent bustles with morning work. Citizens head out to the fields with pitchforks and empty milk jars. First Class women lead the weavers and bakers and cobblers. The scent of good fine bread fills the air. There's a sound of a baby's cry from the nursery, where the mothers care for the infant girls, yet another year passing without a male born, praise Mother God. Apprentices and children make their way up to the Great Hall, where they will have lessons in music, gardening, nursing, and a dozen other skills. All in peace. All in harmony.

Selene leads them down the hill, to the outer edges of the Convent village. Nora is curious as they approach the chicken coop. It is not a place a mother normally visits.

They stop by the outdoor pen. Selene stands calmly, hands clasped behind her back, watching. Nora waits by her side. Chicks flurry about in puffs of yellow. Hens peck at the dirt, kicking up dust and stink. A rooster cocks its way among them.

"I once worked here as an apprentice," Selene says. "Early on there was a rooster I took a liking to. It had magnificent green tailfeathers and crowed like high heaven."

"Not that rooster?" Nora asks.

Selene lets out a laugh. "They don't live that long, even to full age, and this was before you were even born. But the one I liked didn't make it to full age. It was killed."

"That's terrible. What happened?"

"It challenged an older rooster. Bloody mess."

"Why would it do that?"

"Males cannot help themselves. The evil is deep within them, and it comes out as aggression and violence. Ah, look at this one, so proud of its cockscomb. Just watch."

The rooster moves strangely, shuffling toward a hen with a wing outstretched. The hen backs away but the rooster doesn't stop. It leaps forward and lands on the hen. Claws on its back, clucking, flapping. Then the rooster hops off and prances away as the hen composes herself.

Selene sighs. "I learned not to trust their looks. They are vile and most unpleasant. They fight and gloat and foist themselves upon hens just for a cloacal kiss with their papilla."

"Papilla?"

"Have you forgotten your anatomy? It is a little bump of the rooster. They tap it against the hen to fertilize the eggs. Yet, we have no choice but to keep some chicks that will become roosters."

"So we'll have more chickens."

"Yes. It is the way of animals. But Mother God made us capable of far greater in life. We do not need the bump of a papilla. We need only seed. That is why we have long cultivated the gentlest ones, to harvest what we need. It is not a sin for them to be born as they are. But sin slithers into them around twelve years old. We remove the venom from all but the sires, yet we can do even better. Soon we'll need no sires. Soon there will be a last boy."

A last boy. Nora thinks of the baby girls. She cannot remember a boy being born. "How?"

Selene smiles widely, her first smile since she arrived at Nora's door. "We have much to show you, if you become a mother. The Convent is doing amazing things. But we must guard our progress. That is the responsibility of the mothers. We think you might be capable of this."

"Thank you, mother."

Selene fixes a steady gaze on Nora. "Though I hear you have already spent much time with your new captive. His venom has not faded. A mother must never be taken with bright tailfeathers."

"No, of course not. I have only learned songs from him. He will become a fine citizen."

"Good. You might need those new songs. Two will compete tonight to become a mother. You know what will be required?"

"Yes, mother." Nora has seen a competition once before, when she was only a child. Two from First Class performed before the Convent: Valkyrie sang and Selene played the flute. All of First Class and the mothers voted on their selection. Selene won by six votes. "I was there when you won."

"It was a night I'll never forget," Selene says. "But the pressure can be hard. That's why Lilith sent me. We nominated you."

"Thank you, mother."

"Many of us would like for you to win tonight. We have seen how you play. We think you will do well. But some mothers have a different preference."

Nora summons the courage to ask the question, afraid of the answer. "Who will I compete against?"

"Your friend, Eve."

11

♂

Shave

NIGHT PASSES IN TEARS, AND day comes cold and black. The blue sky is out of Jude's sight. The sunlight does not reach him. Smoke still smothers his thoughts. The blast of a shotgun deafens his ears. The loss of mother and home drains him of life.

Still, he treks onward, trying to find a way forward. He knows where he must go. He no longer holds any fascination about the Convent, only disgust and fury. But he feels its pull even stronger now. He has to find out what happened to Esau, the only family he has left. He has to learn what kind of people would do this. Then, maybe, he'll find a way to destroy it. To burn down what left his life in ashes.

He dares not follow the river. It is the way the other woman will likely return to the Convent. He will go a different way, a direct way over hill and valley, as Esau led him only days ago. Was it only days ago? It was a lifetime.

He stops to rest at midday. He sits on a stump and sips

water and stares blankly at the clouds. He looks down at Pa's old shotgun that he brought from the cellar. He tries to eat from his bag of supplies but can't. The pain in his gut allows no hunger.

He trudges on and reaches the fence at dusk. In the distance a bonfire blazes like a torch on the Convent hill, with an ocean of darkness around it. That is a start. Now the fire needs only to spread.

He gazes numbly at a sign: RESTRICTED AREA . . .

He rips it off the fence and throws it to the ground and spits on it. He climbs the fence and makes his way toward the field where he saw the girl, Nora. The smoke lifts when he thinks of her eyes. He can see them clearly, and they tell him that she is different from these people. She wore a red dress. They wore white robes. She wanted to talk. They wanted only to capture and kill. Maybe he will find her again.

By the time he reaches the edge of the field, he is stumbling, legs and heart weary. He still hasn't eaten. Even the thought of sneaking across the field in the night makes him sink inside himself. He is in no shape to go deeper into enemy territory.

Ma's voice speaks to him. *Wait*, it says. *Be patient, Jude. No good comes from the darkness of night.*

Yes. He will rest and eat and then find a way in.

He moves back down the river, wary of sleeping too close. He finds a good thick tree and pitches his hammock high above the ground. He sways and gazes at the stars and listens to the distant sounds. There's music beyond the crickets.

Horns and occasional strings—violin and cello, he thinks. It sounds faint but pleasant. He wonders how bad people can create good music.

Eventually the distant sounds fade and leave him alone with the insects. He tries to imagine ways that Ma could have survived. He tries not to replay the sight of his home burning. He tries not to cry again. But tears fill his eyes as sleep overcomes him.

The morning comes silver and cold. A full moon still hangs over the horizon, a pale remnant of the night.

He forces himself to eat a little, then packs up his hammock and clambers down the tree. He studies the hilltop where the bonfire burned the night before. He looks the opposite way, down the river that runs like a ribbon through the wilderness. Should he flee? How could he stand against the people who took his family?

He doesn't know. But he can't give up. Esau might still be alive.

He follows the river and spots the familiar willow with the canoe hidden underneath. He shivers as he runs his hands along the words engraved in the wood, *The Odyssey*. He wipes away a tear and kneels for a drink. The air smells of snow but it's too early for that. The leaves are still green in the trees, with only faint hints of gold. The gray sky is still.

The river is still, too. Jude glances at his reflection. He looks older. His curls hang in tangles. He feels his chin and the fuzz there. Is it a little darker?

He unzips the leather bag Ma gave him. He takes out the

razor and brush. This isn't the way he imagined his first shave. Pa would've taught him how to do it. The water would've been warm. The mirror without ripples.

A man does what he must, Pa often said.

He starts with the brush and soap. The lather like ice. The reflection blurred. The blade comes toward his neck like a reaper's sickle. It feels cold and severe against his chin. He scrapes carefully. Fine peach-fuzz whiskers cut away and drift lazily in the water, hardly more than motes of dust. It takes only a few sweeps to sheer his chin of any sign of manhood.

It's not enough, he decides.

They shave the boys' heads and make them slaves, one of Esau's friends said. Now that's probably what they are: slaves of the Convent.

Wet and cold and determined, he moves the blade to his hair. Long dark locks fall into the water. He keeps going, stroke by careful stroke, until his head wears only fuzz. He washes off and feels clean but deeply hollow. It wasn't supposed to be this way.

A man does what he must.

He packs up and leaves his bag and shotgun in the hidden canoe, tucked under the willow's veil of leaves. He keeps only the razor, just in case. Best to sneak into the Convent as light and quiet as he can.

12

♀

Funeral

FLICKERING FLAMES LEAP INTO THE night sky. Stars sprawl like diamonds against the infinite black. The Convent's Great Hall stands in pristine white beauty, overlooking the funeral pyre and the crowd around it. The crowd's focus has shifted from the fire to the two girls who stand closest to it.

Soon the two girls will play. Two from First Class. Two best friends, Nora and Eve. And only one will get a chance to become a mother.

It happens so rarely. Once a decade, perhaps.

The twelve mothers rule with such grace and poise that the citizens of the Convent nearly expect them to live forever. The mothers' white hair and wise wrinkles suggest many of them have.

But one named Krystal did not survive last night. The mothers said that she went peacefully in her sleep, from natural causes.

Now her body, once shrouded in white silk and covered in white roses, burns upon the pyre. They know her soul already rejoices in heaven, where the work of the Convent is complete. Where there is only beauty, only joy, all in unison with Mother God.

But here on Earth the work of the Convent must go on. Tonight, as the pyre burns, they will choose a possible replacement.

Possible, Nora reminds herself, because only bearing a child can turn a woman from First Class into a Mother. And what an honor it would be to get that chance. To choose a sire. To bring new life.

She eyes Eve on the other side of the pyre. Her friend's classic beauty radiates—ringlets of dark hair, child-bearing hips. She smiles at Nora. She thinks she will win. But she doesn't know what Nora has learned in recent days.

Nora smiles back, sweet and innocent.

Still, it's a pity they have to compete. Neither of them chose this. It's the Convent's way. When a mother passes, the other mothers tend to nominate young women to take her place. That way, if she conceives, she will have the most years ahead in which to bear children. Nora imagines five, nine, even twelve new lives she could give to the Convent.

But first she has to beat her best friend.

Horns blow to start the ceremony. The eleven mothers encircle Nora and Eve. Firelight dances and gleams on their wise faces.

"It begins," Lilith announces, arms held high, ruby ablaze

at her neck. "We choose the one who creates the most beauty."

A nervous hush spreads in the crowd. Eve, as the older of the two, will play first. Then Nora, followed by brief replies for each. Nora is not surprised to see Eve's choice of the cello. It suits her—deeper and weightier.

Eve plays one of her favorites, a sonata by Brahms, a song Nora has heard a hundred times. Eve performs it masterfully. The crackle of the funeral pyre adds bits of staccato, and she finishes with a grand crescendo.

The crowd claps in approval. The Convent has always loved Eve. Named after the first mother created by Mother God, Eve has always lived into the name. She represents the best in women. Except that Nora is better, in mind and discipline and all that is necessary to be a mother, and so she must win.

Nora remains motionless, waiting, until the applause fades.

When the only sound is the fire, she raises her violin, slow and elegant. Let the world listen. Let the crowd anticipate. Let them savor this moment before they hear a song they've never heard before.

Nora smiles, breathes deep, and starts the Devil's Trill.

The rapid notes singe the air. Every person and every atom seem to bend toward her. Time rushes, as ever, while Nora plays. She relishes the control, savors the attention.

When she draws out the final note, the crowd erupts.

Nora looks to Eve. Her friend gazes at her with awe and a

hint of surprise. The smile on Eve's lips does not reach her eyes.

Again the applause fades.

Eve's brow furrows in concentration. Then she begins her reply. The next piece is elegant, though she misses a note near the beginning. The mistake creates separation between her and the cello, her and the crowd. The applause comes more tepid this time.

This is it, Nora thinks. *My one chance.*

She needs only to be flawless. The Convent loves perfection and order. She had planned on another new piece learned from E11, but it would be an unnecessary risk. Instead, she chooses her favorite song since she was a child.

Clair de Lune.

She plays it gently, in rhythm with the rising moon. Her notes are smooth and clean. She finishes with the composed smile of a master in full command of her craft.

The crowd cheers. Not as loud as for the Trill, but louder than for Eve. Nora takes a deep breath. She has this.

"Well done!" Lilith calls out. "Now we vote. Remember, all eligible must vote, and only once. There will be no discussion. All in favor of Eve, come to her. All in favor of Nora, come to her."

The crowd begins to move. It parts, some splitting to Eve's side of the fire. Others to Nora's, including Lilith and Selene.

It's close, too close. A count will be required.

Nora's stomach sinks as she tries to number those around

her. One, two, three . . . she loses track at nineteen . . . she guesses there are at least forty. On Eve's side she counts ten, twenty, thirty . . .

The mothers huddle in the middle, deliberating. They govern all things of the Convent, but not this. For the selection of the next mother they serve only to count and declare the winner.

The mothers part and Lilith raises her arms. "You have chosen the next mother."

Horns blow again, louder. Nora's chest feels tight.

Lilith steps toward her. "Nora!"

The crowd cheers and surrounds her and places their hands on her. Supporting, loving. It is the Convent's way.

A group parts before her and Eve is there.

"You earned it," she says. "Congratulations."

Nora bows deeply, truly. "Thank you, Eve. You'll be next."

Eve embraces her and whispers in her ear. "I'm counting on it."

Nora only smiles in return, masking her unease. This is not final. She must conceive to cement her place. Eve will be ready if she does not.

But the crowd has no such hesitation. They sweep her up in celebration. There will be more music tonight. There will be feasting. It is a funeral and a wedding. One mother is gone, but another will rise, married to the Convent, dedicated to their peace and to bringing new life.

13

♂

Infiltrate

HEAD SHAVED AND HEART SHORN, Jude follows the river until he reaches the place where he first saw the girl. He creeps to the edge of the field and watches until he's sure there's no one around. No girl. Not even a cow.

He moves like a ghost through the high grass, leaving a vivid green line through the silver sea of dew. No going back now.

He hurries into the barn. Cows eye him from their stalls. Manure smells thick as sour syrup in the air.

He hears faint singing in the distance. The rhythmic chant echoes eerily in the barn. The cows look as eager as cows can. Jude guesses whoever it is will come this way. Cows will be fed. He climbs a ladder to a loft of hay bales to get a better look.

Through a crack in the faded barnwood wall he sees two people cresting the hill from the opposite way he came. They're coming straight for the barn from the Convent. But they're not the strange women he saw, or the girl.

They wear plain brown cloaks with hoods up. They move like boys. And they sound . . . happy.

Jude slips to the back of the loft and wedges behind hay bales, pressed tight against the wall. The two singing voices swell into the barn and reverberate around him. Words become clear.

Hi-ho, hi-ho, it's off to milk we go,
A brand new day,
We work and play,
To make the Convent glow.

Jude recognizes the tune from an old fairy tale. Pa used to whistle it as he worked. These new words almost make him laugh, so frivolous, so false.

The singing stops.

"Pat, they look hungry today," a boy calls out. "Might take four or five bales."

The ladder rattles. Jude moves as far back as he can, hiding in the shadows of the loft.

A head appears over the ledge. It's a boy with eyes as calm as river stones. He moves to the hay and grabs a bale by the string holding it together. He grunts as he tries to lift it, then lets it fall. Straw dust flutters up into the air. It's too heavy for him. He steps over it and starts to push instead. Slowly it slides across the floor. When the boy gets it to the edge, he kicks it over to the ground of the barn below.

"One!" he calls out, then turns back. He tosses back his hood and reveals a head of close-shaved hair, like Jude's. He wipes sweat from his brow and starts to push the next bale over.

He's shorter than Jude, but not by much. He should be able to lift a bale of hay. Jude waits and thinks until the third bale has been shoved over and by then he knows: he has to act.

When the boy comes for the fourth bale and starts to slide it with his back turned, Jude jumps him.

The boy grunts but doesn't shout.

Jude holds the razor blade to his throat and whispers, "Don't make a noise. Don't move."

The boy contorts his back like a cat dunked in a cold bath.

"Just do what I say and I won't kill ya," Jude says. "Blink twice if you understand."

The boy blinks twice and Jude almost smiles. He's not proud of lying—because he'd never kill the boy—but he's sure glad this is working. For now.

"Pat?" a voice calls out from below.

"Tell him ya fell," Jude whispers urgently an inch from the boy's ear. "Say it's no problem. Next bale is comin'."

The boy says it exactly as Jude asked.

Jude tosses the bale down and comes back and holds up the razor and tells the boy to undress.

The boy looks at Jude like he's crazy. Jude figures maybe he *is* a little crazy right now, which is probably why the boy does as he's told. Jude hauls another bale over the edge. Then he rushes back, strips quickly, and puts on the boy's clothes. The fit's not bad.

Jude doubts the boy will try anything but to be safe he ties the boy's wrists and ankles together behind his bare back. He starts to tie a cloth over the boy's mouth but hesitates.

"Hey, what's that boy's name down there?" Jude asks.

"J8, or Jo. But it's not a boy. Neither am I."

"Huh?" Jude glances down between the boy's legs. "Sure looks like it to me."

"We're citizens."

"Okay, whatever. Tell me what you're supposed to do next."

"We take the cows out to the pasture and deliver milk to the mothers. We usually sing, too."

"Who are the mothers?"

"Our leaders. Who are *you*?"

"A boy. Your people caught my friends."

"The wild men?"

"You know about them?"

"I saw four of them brought in a few days ago. Dirty and hairy and gross. Praise Mother God they won't trouble us anymore. Their type gets harvested and put to rest. Not everyone gets to be a citizen like me."

Put to rest. Esau.

The boy's tone is clear, but Jude doesn't want to believe it. "How are they put to rest?"

"I'm sure it's gentle. The mothers are always gentle."

Jude holds the razor blade to the boy's neck. "That's a lie. There's nothing gentle about killing."

The boy shakes his head, looking scared, but he doesn't deny it. Jude feels sick to his stomach.

What if they killed Esau, like they killed Ma . . .

"Pat?" the boy calls out from below. "You okay up there?"

"Silence," Jude whispers to the boy. He raises his voice an octave, trying to match his captive's. "Just one more bale!"

"We *got* plenty."

"Oh okay. Be right down."

Jude doesn't have time to think. It's time for action. He ties the cloth over the boy's mouth. "You're going to stay here quiet as a rock till sundown. Got it?"

The boy nods and lies there, passive and obedient. He doesn't even struggle.

Jude pulls his hood up and climbs down to the ladder. His heart is racing as he looks to the other boy. The boy wears the same brown clothes as Jude, with his hood up. He's tossing hay into the cow's stalls with a pitchfork. He gives Jude only a passing glance.

"You sure took your time today," the boy says.

Jude steadies himself. This is working. And if it stops working, he has a weapon. "Sorry, I'm feeling tired."

"You *sound* tired. You push yourself too hard lifting those bales. Better to slide them like I said. Take the easy way. Here, take this bucket and milk Bessie. I'll lead the others out."

Jude takes the bucket and scans the stalls and notices little signs outside each one. They bear letters in Latin. Jude thinks of all the times he complained to Ma about learning a dead language. Now he breathes a sigh of relief. He goes to the last stall marked with *Beta* and opens the gate. There's a large black and white cow, with a stool beside it. He sits and thanks Ma again for teaching him how to milk. He takes hold of the soft udder and squeezes one fistful at a time.

Soon the other boy passes by him with a cart of glass jars full of milk. "See you soon," the boy says cheerfully. "We'll be down by the river."

As the bucket fills, a sense of unease crawls over Jude. *It's not a boy*, the boy said. *Neither am I*. It doesn't make sense. What are they if not boys? He said they're citizens, but then why are they acting so docile? And who do they think Mother God is? *Harvested, put to rest*. He prays Esau has survived, somehow.

When the pail is mostly full, Jude uses a funnel to pour the milk into two glass jars and goes outside. The other boy waves him over. Jude puts his jars beside the others in the cart.

"Forget something?" the boy asks, looking past Jude to the barn.

"Bessie?" Jude asks, keeping his hood drawn tight.

"Well yeah! You sure are spacey this morning. Worried about the ceremony?"

"I guess so."

"You'll play great. Yes, there will be a crowd and a new mother and the chance to be a sire and all that, but no one's practiced minuets as hard as you. I wish I had half your skill on the violin."

"Thanks," Jude says, in disbelief. For a moment he thinks the other boy sees who he really is, but then he realizes the boy he just tied up must play the violin, like him. He remembers the music from the night before. Maybe they all play. Maybe this is his chance to get inside and find a way to fight against this terrible place.

"Well, don't just stand there. Go get Bessie and let's get this milk delivered to the Convent."

Jude does as he's told, and the boy sings behind him.

Hi-ho, hi-ho, it's off to milk we go.

14

♀

Interrogate

NORA STUDIES THE CITIZEN in the center of the room. They have played violin together for several days now, before and after Nora's victory with the Devil's Trill.

The citizen no longer shows such impatience and anger. No longer stares at Nora's chest. It's as it should be, Nora knows, but part of her senses a difference in the music, too. Less vibrant, less powerful. Not that Nora would ever miss the wildness, but she senses that time is running short. The mothers say it can take a month after the procedure for the trouble to fade from the body.

And tonight Nora will choose a sire. It can't be this citizen, but she might still learn from E11.

Nora leans closer, eye to eye. "How did your family end up in the wild?"

"I don't know," E11 says.

"Surely your Ma and Pa told you something about their lives."

"They were born in a city."

"What was it called?"

"I don't know."

"Didn't you ask?"

"Sure. They didn't like to talk about it."

"Why did they leave?"

"How should I know?" The citizen huffs in annoyance. "You asked me that already. Three times."

Nora crosses her arms. "And you haven't answered me."

"What's the point of all this?"

"We need to understand our new citizens."

"*Understand?*" E11 surges to its feet so fast the chair falls back and clatters on the stone floor. Its fist clamps over Nora's arm like an iron vice.

"Is everything okay?" a guard calls from outside the door.

"Yes," Nora calls back. She meets the citizen's stare, ignoring the pain of its grip, heart aflutter at its energy. This could be a breakthrough.

"Go on," she whispers.

"Understand *this*," E11 snarls. "You took my Pa. You kidnapped me. Now you lock me up. Shackle me. Inject me with something. Call me *E11* and *it*. Make me sit here and play violin and answer your stupid questions. Well *I* have questions. Who are you people? What is this sick game? What do you want from me?"

Nora eyes the white-knuckled hand clutching her arm. Her voice comes out softly, "Let me go?"

The fist slowly releases.

"Come here, I want to show you something." Nora moves to the small window.

The citizen follows. Together they look out over the Convent. It is another glorious day. Pairs of hooded citizens go about their work amidst the orderly white buildings. In the distance two of them approach from the fields with a cart of milk jars. One of the mothers, clad in white, leads a group of apprentices up the hill toward the Great Hall. Voices sing softly from different directions, overlapping in a gentle tapestry.

"This is your home now," Nora says. "We live in peace. Harmony. Beauty. Joy."

"No," the citizen replies, though without anger. "I don't want this. If you won't let me go, it's a prison."

Nora meets the citizen's eyes and smiles. "Give it time."

"I don't want time . . ."

She hears defeat in its voice. The mothers say this is the first stage for a new citizen. The old must die. New life will grow. "The sooner you accept your place here, the sooner you'll be free."

"I'm only free in the wild."

"Why did your family go there?"

The citizen stiffens, resistance returning. "I don't know."

Nora sighs in disappointment. "This could be your final chance to answer me. Your next questioner may not be so gentle."

"I've told you what I know."

"Very well. Goodbye, E11."

Nora turns and leaves without a glance back. She pauses outside the room with her back to the door. The First Class guards at her side are still as statues.

I was so close, she thinks. The treatments will have their effect. The citizen will change. It will conform and accept its place, or it will be removed. She should be pleased. Her first capture can be a good citizen. It could have been a sire, even for her, if only she'd caught it younger. Still, once its T is fully gone, E11 will serve the First Class, Nora feels sure. An honorable and good life for one of such talent and energy.

She hopes to find something similar in a sire.

Tonight she'll have to decide. She's made a capture, she's been chosen, and she's ready to become a mother. If only she can find the right sire. There are few who are eligible. Still, she'll have her choice among those who fit the Convent's standards. Their testing is scrupulous.

Gentle spirit.

Loving soul.

Dextrous hands.

Pliable mind.

Tall. Handsome. Like that wild boy who escaped . . .

No, Nora smiles to herself. The Convent would never stipulate physical requirements. They are too advanced for that. But in every session with E11 she's affected by its physical presence. The grip on her arm was so strong, yet so smooth with the violin.

Nora almost blushes, remembering the guards beside her. She needs space to think. She begins to walk. Her long strides take her down the red-carpet halls and outside. The courtyard is radiant in sunlight. Across from her the Convent's Great Hall rises, a white stone monument of peace. The majestic steeple bears at its top a circle with a cross beneath it—the symbol of woman, the sign of fulfillment.

Birds swoop down from the high-pitched ceiling to rest in the oak trees around the Great Hall. They sing and call to each other across the square, the hum of happy music. A flock soars off as a shadowy mass against the blue sky.

What joy for these little creatures to raise their voices and fly as one, Nora thinks. She wonders at how they keep peace among their chaos. They even mate by choice, unlike the pitiful hens with the rooster. Humans are made for more, Selene said. Nora does not doubt it. E11 proves the danger of T, of its aggressive spirit. The new citizen makes her feel too . . . exposed, vulnerable.

Nora will recommend more analysis. The mothers should assess E11's genetic data further. Nora wants to learn how they do it, but she needs to be a true mother first. That's why she must focus on the decision tonight.

She walks down the Convent's main street toward her dormitory room. She admires the neat rows of rosebushes, still in bloom even as fall's coolness touches the air. Others are about, handling their daily business. Two young girls sit on the stairs of a white brick building practicing with their violins. Scratchy but the form is there. They will learn in time.

She passes the pair of citizens she saw before, hauling the cart of milk jars. One of them looks at her, and the gaze lingers a moment too long. A chill goes down her spine. As if she's seen the citizen before.

She glances toward the window where E11 is. It can't be. She looks back, but the citizens have already moved along with their cart.

Set the distraction aside. Selene warned her, and the mothers always know best. She should not be surprised if they look familiar. It is good for the citizens to look alike.

She enters her building and goes to her room. It's her favorite time of day—the golden afternoon. She should have a little time before Eve comes to help her prepare for the ceremony.

Sitting at her desk, she gazes at the cluster of fresh-cut pink roses. Her favorite. She writes a summary note for the mothers.

E11 has potential. Too much T still interferes with its gifts. Reveals little of its past. Further assessment required. Estimated time for compliance . . .

Nora hesitates. All should conform in time. Most accept their place soon after their T is gone. Perhaps a month. But she's read of some new citizens taking six months. How long for E11?

Her pen draws it out carefully: *one year.*

It is an extreme but simple prognosis. The kind the mothers will appreciate. Nora has done her job.

She gazes out at the green and faintly golden leaves on the trees. Some fall and swirl and dance. Wind jerks a few violently, as if in tune to the Devil's Trill.

You should see my brother, E11 said.

Nora swallows. The citizen who stared at her had the same wildness as E11. But no. Not possible. Deep breaths.

She goes to her bed and curls up. Sleep comes.

A knock on the door wakes her. She rises and collects herself. The light has barely shifted. She couldn't have napped for more than an hour.

The door opens and Eve enters.

"Beauty sleep?" her friend asks. "I've been tired since last night, too. But you should be excited. Tonight's your big night."

Nora yawns and stretches. "The new citizen tired me."

"Neophytes are renowned for troubling us. But come now. Let me work my magic."

Nora shuffles to the corner of the room, before the standing mirror. She smiles at Eve's reflection behind her shoulder.

"I think I'll wear white tonight," Nora says.

"White for sure. Brilliant with your new emerald." Eve moves to the armoire and pulls out a new dress that dazzles even as it hangs without form. "You'll impress even the mothers in this."

Nora smiles as Eve goes to work dressing her and doing her hair. But as she looks at her own face she knows the smile is not full. She's still shaken by E11 and the citizen she passed with the milk cart. Let her unease be fuel for her fire when she plays tonight. Like the mothers before her, she will choose her sire and dispel the masculine curse with beauty.

15

♂

Religion

JUDE PULLS THE MILK CART like a loyal mule. The other boy sings cheerfully, carefree as a bird, as they pass through the pillars marking the Convent's entrance. Jude stays silent. He told the boy he needed to prepare in his mind for tonight's ceremony. Whatever that means, the boy seemed to believe him.

Now, among the enemy, Jude's nerves fray. What if his ruse collapses? A bee buzzes past his nose and he almost runs.

Stay cool, Jude.

Everything Jude had imagined about the Convent crumbles under reality. The buildings around him have brick walls so clean and white that they shine. The doors and shutters are painted crimson red. The roofs are orderly gray slate. Trimmed rows of bushes line the main road up the hill to a huge cathedral. It stands so tall that the other buildings, even the ancient oak trees, seem to bow down before it. A large icon rises above its steeply pitched roof and looms over the Convent like a false moon.

It's all stunning, even beautiful. But how can such beauty be mixed with such evil? He pulls his gaze down from the buildings around him and she's there.

The girl. Nora.

She comes from the hill above, a stone's throw away, but moving gracefully toward him. For a moment, he almost steps toward her, drawn by her.

No. She'll recognize me. She's the enemy.

He forces himself to look away and keep moving with the cart. As they pass her, Jude summons every ounce of discipline to hold his tongue, fighting down his curiosity and knowing a word could mean capture. She continues down the hill, and his eyes follow her as she goes.

"Hey, what are you doing?" the boy asks, setting down his side of the cart. "We're almost there."

Jude turns. The boy has stepped off the main path and faces stairs leading up to one of the buildings.

"Right, sorry," Jude says.

"You're sure acting funny today," the boy says with a laugh. "You better take a nap or something."

Jude follows him into the building. It's austere inside, matching the outside with plain, white-painted walls. The floor is dark polished wood. Jude and the boy move down a long hallway past identical doors. Each one has the same crimson color and a number set in the center.

The boy suddenly stops. The door has the number 8.

"Earth to P8," the boy says.

Jude follows his gaze to the door and reaches for the handle.

"Um, wrong room." The boy laughs again but this time there's unease in it. "You want me to ask a nurse to come?"

Jude keeps his head down, retreating within his hood. "Just tired," he mumbles. "Still thinking about tonight. Nervous, I guess."

"Oh I know that," the boy says. "Look, I'll take care of picking up the empty bottles this afternoon. You sleep. You've got the best chance of all of us tonight. And it will be your only chance. There aren't many citizens left who are younger than us, and they look up to you. We're all counting on you."

"Thanks." Jude's appreciation is not entirely fake. He's baffled by the boy's naivety and kindness.

He goes back to the prior door, number 7. It opens, and the boy waves and moves on down the hall.

Inside is a simple, small room. White walls and ceiling. A bed and a desk. There's a small alcove with a window with a rounded top and a view of a garden. It's all cleaner and nicer than the room he grew up in—the same way a bare plate compares to one heaped with warm food.

He sits by the window and watches. The people outside move from place to place with purpose. They are mostly girls in dresses of all different colors. Several of them carry instruments, as if going to or from a lesson. There's a steady, muffled sound of faint music in the air, as if dozens practice in separate rooms. The only boys he sees are dressed in the same plain brown clothes that he wears. Some of them, too, carry instruments. But most go about doing chores as if watched. Every older woman he sees walks with other women, talking and smiling as if this is the most normal place in the world. He wonders if he will see Nora again, but she does not appear.

Bells ring from up on the hill, probably from the building at the top. The steady sound of practice music falls silent. The bells chime four times. Jude figures it's 4 o'clock.

At the last chime, a sound plays inside the room. Jude turns and notices a small screen set into the wall at the foot of the bed. It was dark before. Now the screen shows moving images. He's read about these devices but never seen one in person.

He moves closer and watches, amazed, as a video plays. It shows rows and rows of soldiers. All men in identical military attires. They wear a symbol on their shoulder. Jude recognizes it as a swastika.

The video leaps into action, cutting quickly from scene to scene. There's a battle showing men shot and blown to pieces by bombs. There's a hospital with nurses carefully tending to bloody and wounded men. There's an explosion the size of a mountain.

The screen goes black again. Words appear in white:
Create a world of peace,
Where wars and fightings cease.
The letters fade. The room is quiet and still.

Jude pulls himself away from the screen in a daze. He moves to the desk and sits. A book lies there. It's a journal with a plain cover and careful handwritten script inside. About half of the pages have been used. The latest page has verses of poems. The first has a large X scribbled over it.

Milk the cows at dawn
Udder like a tactile prawn
Feed the mothers milk
May the Convent live long.

Jude thinks the poem is crap, but it disturbs him. The boy he tied up in the barn really believed this. The other poems, even the ones that haven't been scribbled out, are no better.

Twelve mothers birth us.
One brought me to life.
To peace, never strife.

The more Jude reads, the sicker he feels. The boy is brainwashed. He writes about the videos that are played. He fears the world outside. He seems content in this place. Tending the cows. Practicing music. Sleeping and eating and doing it all over again, day after day. He knows nothing of heroes or adventure. No wonder the boy didn't put up a fight in the barn. He's got as much spine as a jellyfish.

Jude turns back to the journal's first page. Inside the cover there's a page with elegant gold foil font at the top—*The Holy Word of the Convent, An Excerpt.*

Large, flowing calligraphy fills the rest of the page:

In the beginning Mother God created the heavens and the earth and all that is in it. She created the first human mother,

Eve, in her own image, to bring forth life to the Convent. In perfect obedience, Eve bore two children.

The first child was a daughter born in Mother God's image. Eve saw that she was good and named her Lilith.

The second child was born malformed by the devil. Eve saw that he was evil and named him Adam.

The boy child attempted to murder the daughter child. Eve and Lilith, mother and daughter, together prevailed and subdued Adam. In love they forgave and cared for the boy child and used his seed to bring forth more children. Half again were beautiful, and the other half corrupted. War and destruction followed the corrupted children wherever they sojourned until twelve mothers united to establish the Convent, flowing with milk and honey.

Jude, awestruck by this grand myth, notes that the boy has underlined the word milk. The text continues.

The twelve mothers rescued the corrupted children from the devil's evil. They preserved enough seed to create life, for the daughters are fruitful and multiply. Thus the mothers shall preserve the earth until Eve shall come again.

Outside the Convent, Mother God and the devil still struggle. War rages and evil reigns, bringing death. The Convent alone shines until all shall be redeemed as daughters in eternity. In heaven there shall be no corrupted children nor weeping nor fighting nor pain. All shall be daughters, and all shall live in paradise everlasting.

Jude's hands shake as he closes the journal. He remembers what Ma taught him, words that he's read over and over: *God created them male and female.*

Mind reeling, Jude wants to run away while he still can. But he thinks of Ma, of Pa, of Esau. *The corrupted child, my brother.* No, wild as Esau was, there was good in him.

Now his family is gone. His home is cinders.

All he has left is to keep swimming in the evil current until he finds a way to stop it for good.

16

♀

Ceremony

NORA ENTERS THE GREAT HALL like a bride entering a cathedral. Trumpets announce her entry. Citizens and apprentices turn to watch her from the pews, each decorated with glorious bouquets of roses, red and white. Horns crescendo and then cease in unison.

An expectant silence falls. All eyes fixed on her.

She takes her first step with her chin up. Then another step. Slow and steady. The white train of her dress trails on the red carpet. She imagines the thoughts of those she passes, surely full of respect and love. Then she glances at her friend, Eve.

Don't trip, Eve whispered.

Nora could almost laugh. Only the thought of tripping would threaten her now. She brushes her friend's words aside. Much as Eve would like to be in her position, Eve helped her prepare. She supports her. Everyone does. It is the Convent's way.

This is my moment, our *moment, for the Convent.*

She strides forward in confidence, keeping her eyes on the mothers and suitors who await in the front.

The mothers have prepared Nora for this since the day she was born. She admires their wisdom. They were once as she was, and she will become what they are. This is the cycle of life. This is the Convent's majesty.

The mothers even taught her about weddings. They were events of the old, corrupted world, now known for their depravity, when a man and woman would vow to marry and love each other until death do them part. It never worked, of course. The men could never be trusted, try as a woman might. Such evils, praise the mothers, have been replaced by this.

She comes to a stop before the eleven elegant women in white. She bows low and keeps her eyes on the red carpet beneath her feet. She must be humble, even now, especially now.

"Who comes before us?" the mothers ask together.

Nora replies, "One the Convent chooses as mother."

"Rise."

Nora stands as straight and tall as she can. The mothers part and reveal a man who waits behind them, wearing a purple robe and kneeling at the center of the stage. A sire.

He looks up at Nora with dark eyes.

A wave of unease ripples within her. She has seen a sire only a few times before, at ceremonies like this, but never this close. It is good that they keep these men removed to their own quarters. Their very presence is danger. Even this one, a tame example, has testosterone boiling inside him. No wonder he reminds her so much of the boy she captured, except fully grown and bearded.

She steels herself, moves forward, and holds out her hand.

He kisses it, whiskers rough against her smooth skin.

The ancient words come to her lips, words she's practiced a hundred times. "The Convent has need of new life. Our world has need of mothers. I offer myself to the Convent's service. What do you offer me?"

"My only value is my seed." His low voice disturbs her, even if he speaks the correct words. "Mine has already been given. My kind will offer you another."

"I will choose the best of your kind," Nora says, continuing the ritual.

"We exist to serve." The man bows his head to the floor.

Nora turns away from him, relieved to be done with this part. Hundreds watch her eagerly. Their silence is like a womb, ready to give birth to life.

"We have chosen your suitors," the mothers say.

"Show them to me," Nora replies.

The mothers motion to the citizens in the first pew. They step up to the stage and form a line, with six on either side of the kneeling sire. Twelve total. Each one is near her age. They are modest, dressed alike in brown. Heads shaved, quiet eyes, gentle spirits—but still able to offer seed. The mothers have carefully bred and tested and groomed these citizens. This is the best the Convent has to offer. There can be no wrong choice.

Yet Nora still yearns to study them. She has to find the best fit, for the Convent and for her. They must share their gifts with all.

"I accept the suitors," she says, as she knows she must.

"Let one prove the value of its seed," the mothers reply.

The citizens move back to their pew.

Nora faces the crowd again. "Bring my instrument."

A citizen hurries to her with the violin, then hurries away. Nora holds it calmly, relishing the comfort it gives her. Music is one thing she can always control.

With every eye riveted on her, she lifts her violin. She takes a deep breath. She smells the roses filling the room, fragrant as life itself. Every ounce of energy is here. Every source of life. One of these suitors will donate seed. Let them glimpse the brilliant progeny that could be theirs. Let them earn the right.

She begins to play.

17

♂

Challenger

IT'S HER. THE REAL LIVE GIRL. The first one Jude saw, the one he'll never forget. She plays the fiddle like a whirlwind on the stage. She twists and churns, her white dress flowing around her like clouds in the wind. Something about her form, her slender arms and short pixie hair, mesmerizes Jude in his front row seat.

The girl finishes and applause washes over her, gentle as spring rain. Jude glances behind him at the gelded boys clapping placidly, surrounded by stupidly large bunches of flowers. They all cheer as if it's their duty.

She deserves more than this, Jude thinks. She deserves a standing ovation, whoops and hollers. Her performance of the Devil's Trill would have made Esau proud, even Tartini himself.

As the cheering fades, brown-cloaked boys scurry into motion around Jude. He knows little about how this is supposed to work. But he knows he's lucky. The boy he tied up had apparently been chosen to perform and compete to be a suitor. And now he understands that his real live girl will be the one who chooses.

Suddenly Jude is sure of one thing. He must win this. He will show her and the Convent real, untamed music. No matter that she's apparently a young queen in a white dress, a tornado with a fiddle. Providence pulled Jude into this. There's no other explaining it—the loss of Esau and Ma and his home, his luck in sneaking into this place, and now, a competition over the one thing in life that he's best at.

You're my virtuoso, Ma said. She taught him from diapers, as if she knew his destiny would require this. And now he can win this competition because he's different than the others.

He can see it in their faces. They don't even call themselves boys. They have no inner fire, no vibrance. Jude figures they've been suppressed all their lives. Jude doesn't know how or why, but he knows he has a spark they don't. Maybe he'll win and break this gelded empire.

Servant boys carry a variety of instruments and distribute them to the suitors on the first row. Jude counts five fiddles, three cellos, two flutes, a trumpet, and a bass.

No way a woodwind wins this.

He studies the fiddle that a boy handed to him. Rich, amber curves. Pristine pegs and hollows. Warmth and energy flows from the wood into his hands and arms and core. It's a masterpiece beyond anything he's ever seen, much less touched. He can hardly believe he'll get to play it.

"The first suitor may approach," the girl says from the

stage.

A boy at the far end of the row rises and moves forward. As he does, the girl glides to the chair where the man sat earlier. He's been kneeling prostrate with his head on the ground, palms to the floor, as if he decided to die on the spot. It's one of the weirdest things Jude's ever seen. Probably meant to be some kind of example for the boys or something. Jude didn't get a good look at the man's face, but it hardly seems to matter. He seems to be only décor.

The boy stands at center stage. His fingers fidget over his fiddle like a cat prancing over water.

"Why do you wait?" the girl asks.

"Yes, sorry," he squeaks, then starts to play. It takes three notes for Jude to know this boy won't have a chance. He's playing an old folk tune, and he's got no spirit.

The boy plays for about two minutes, then returns to his seat.

The next suitor plays a sad drivel on the flute. He's droning on when the lights suddenly blink off and then on again.

The girl says, "Your time is up."

The next suitors play in the same fashion, one at a time, for a couple minutes each. There's no applause for any of them. The vast room is awkwardly quiet as they progress in single file with mechanical bursts of sound. Jude imagines them as a conveyor belt of boys, processed and stamped, thank you very much.

The fifth boy stands a head taller than the rest of them.

He plays cello, and he's not bad. It's a rendition of Mendelssohn's Song Without Words, smooth and subdued.

When he finishes, the girl says, "You may remain."

The boy takes his cello, with a smug smile, to the side of the stage. Another suitor comes without delay. His fiddle doesn't cut it. He's dismissed promptly.

Jude likes the eighth player on bass. He has more vibrance than the others, even if he's the size of a ten-year-old. The massive instrument looks like it could squash him. The lights blink off and on for him, cutting his piece short. Still, the girl asks him to stay. That's two out of eight.

And two more to go before Jude, who's next to last.

The ninth makes the cut with his fiddle.

The tenth boy nearly stumbles getting his cello up on the stage. He places his bow on the strings. He hesitates. He takes a shallow breath and his elbow jerks. From the first note—a creaky E—Jude knows this one won't be moving on.

The boy steps off the stage. Jude is up.

He follows the others' examples and steps to the stage. With a quick bow to the girl, more nervous than he intended, he raises his fiddle. This is his first chance to test the tune. None of the others did it, but he can't resist. He plays the A string, tweaks it slightly.

The girl makes a cough.

Jude meets her eyes. She melts his confidence. She looks displeased, maybe uneasy.

He finishes the rest of the tuning faster than he'd like. A few seconds only, but he suddenly fears his timer is running.

Gazing out at all these women, these witches, seals Jude's decision on the song: Witch's Dance by Paganini.

Deep breath. Eyes on the strings. Imagine Ma listening.

Go.

He launches into the height of the chorus. He loses himself in the notes and sways to the dancing rhythm. He forgets the audience and the Convent. The music is all there is. It flows out of him like water from a spring, clear and true and natural. But also like a spring, it took ages to produce this—shifts within Jude's body and mind like the shifts of the earth's crust, allowing the overflow of this clarity, this beauty.

The light cuts off as he lets the final note linger and vibrate. Jude gazes out like breaking the surface of the water for air. That's two minutes. The timing of the finale was perfect.

The girl stares at him with an odd look in her eyes.

Jude's heart climbs up to his throat, pulsing intensely, choking his very breath. Moments pass like eons.

Did I do something wrong?

Does she know I don't belong?

Does she recognize me?

"You may remain," the girl says, voice like ice.

The words jerk Jude out of his trance. He bows and joins the small group of boys who will move on.

The last suitor misses the cut. Only four remain.

18

♀

Suitor

NORA PACES BEFORE THE FOUR suitors. Only four. She'd expected to narrow down the pool to eight or nine, at least six. Now she must choose among four.

It takes only one.

She remembers to smile. How lovely to see all these musicians! What a delight for hundreds to gather in the Great Hall to witness beauty. It's a shame some will lose, yes, but the mothers say it's the only way. They must, generation by generation, collect the best and cull the worst of humankind. And what progress they've made!

The sea of gentle, admiring faces. She looks to the section of the youngest girls, children and students, looking up to her. There are no males of those young ages. Maybe the suitors are all that's left. She must choose wisely.

They wait with bated breath for the next test: duets. All will want to see the suitor who will match the new mother-to-be. All yearn to know which seed will bring new life to the Convent. The mothers prepared her for this. "I passed on my first four," one mother told her. "Take your time."

Nora stops before the last suitor she picked—the one whose song made the hairs on her neck stand up—and resolves to save it for last. This one unnerves her, even if it has the most talent.

She points her bow at the suitor who barely made it.

The tiny bass player steps forward like a shy mouse. With a grunt it lifts the bass and settles into position beside Nora, facing the crowd.

"A minuet in G," Nora announces.

Their eyes meet, the suitor nods, and Nora begins.

The bass player tries quickly to join her, to follow, but misses a few notes early and never recovers. Too nervous, too small.

The Convent deserves better than that.

She dismisses the suitor, who scurries off the stage to tepid applause. Nice try, the audience suggests. Perhaps the mouse should have chosen a smaller instrument.

Nora picks the tallest suitor to go next. *The handsome one,* she realizes. It has flaxen hair and bright blue eyes, not that it matters. What matters is if the citizen fits. Part of Nora hopes it does.

"Martinu's Duo," she announces.

The suitor's eyes light up, receiving the subtle complement. This is a song for cello to begin. The suitor doesn't hesitate. Its long arms ably bring the bow into motion, drawing rich sound from the standing instrument.

Nora easily meets the pace and tone. Neither fast nor slow, but steady. She wants to like it. The suitor is handsome and tall. But there's something dull about the performance, almost mechanical.

They finish smoothly, in sync. The suitor remains an option. With a twirl of her bow, she motions for the cello player to stay on stage. The crowd gives its loudest cheer yet. They know this could be the one. Nora wishes she felt more sure.

The third suitor approaches with a violin. This one looks younger than the others. Its gentle green eyes glance shyly at Nora. She responds with an amused grin. *Would the Convent value more green eyes? Would I?*

The suitor smiles back so wide that its ears fidget. Such big ears, Nora thinks, not that it matters. Not that it would lead her to choose a song played so often it numbs the Convent.

"Canon in D," she announces.

She begins and the suitor follows smoothly. The notes are right but lack the polish that comes only from confident repetition. This suitor needs more time. Certain she would pick the tall cello player between the two, she dismisses the violin player to faint applause.

One suitor to go. Nora turns to the last boy.

Not boy—suitor! She corrects herself, shocked at the word creeping into her thoughts. A boy is an artifact of history and of the broken world outside the Convent. Here, there are no *boys*. There are only citizens and suitors and sires.

The suitor strides forward without waiting for her to beckon, as if clueless of protocol. Its movements hint at wildness, or maybe it's just uncouth. Nora feels struck with a familiarity about the suitor. *Another one who reminds me of E11*, she thinks. The one too wild to tame. Safer to geld. This suitor could be the same.

Nora knows from the impressive first performance that the suitor can play fast and well. But can it play slow, with emotion? She chooses an easier piece, and one of her favorites.

"Waltz, by Brahms," she says.

She starts quiet and slow as a sunrise. She knows the piece so well she can study the suitor even as she plays. She looks for an expression. She sees nothing but calm.

The suitor lets her play a full ten notes without joining.

It unnerves Nora. Surely the suitor knows the song. Every child of the Convent knows Waltz by age ten. It's standard. It's easy. Yet the suitor watches her curiously, as if beholding a creature never seen before.

She's nearly a minute into the piece when, springing from ambush, the suitor begins to play. It does not follow her lead. There's a quick trill of notes so fast that Nora nearly loses her place in Waltz, of all songs.

By the end of the next measure the boy—*suitor!*—has taken over. The quick staccato pierces through her long notes with the precision of a sewing machine creating an intricate pattern.

Nora forces herself to stay calm, to play steady until the

finish. When the last note fades, applause surges from the crowd. In the midst of it Nora retreats inside herself and marvels at a rising feeling she's never encountered like this: astonishment.

Careful, she tells herself. *Don't be hasty.*

This suitor has spirit, but perhaps too much. She looks to the taller suitor with the cello. Its raised chin suggests complete confidence. Perhaps too much confidence.

She catches the eyes of Eve in the crowd. Her friend's pretty grin seems to say: *Of course you'd pick the cocky ones.*

Nora raises her hands, and the applause fades. "We have reached the final performance," she announces. She faces the two suitors. "You each play one minute, and the other attempts to repeat the performance. Three turns each."

They do not respond, but they look eager.

She points to the taller one. "You, begin."

The suitor moves into position with the cello. Back straight, long limbs graceful, as the suitor sits on the edge of a chair. The bow flows into motion, drawing a rich, rhythmic sound from the instrument. It's easy to listen to. The type of song that could play in the background, over and over, without notice.

The sound fades.

The other suitor with the violin steps up and faces the seated cello. It plays the same song, with a touch more speed and energy. The suitor's notes are flawless, but for this piece, the violin lacks the depth of the cello. A savvy song choice by the cello player. Nora considers it a draw.

"Now your choice," she says to the suitor with the violin.

The suitor grins and plays the song Nora has just learned: Devil's Trill. The sound is so much like E11's. As the notes dance out of the suitor's instrument, Nora loses herself in the suitor's dark green eyes. And there, amidst the wild sound, amidst the storm, the memory flashes before Nora.

She was kneeling with the elastrator when she heard the noise in the forest. She looked up and saw him.

The boy in the woods.

This is not a suitor.

This is the wild one who got away.

She looks into *his* eyes and hears *his* song and knows *he* must be E11's brother. His shaved head and Convent attire hid the truth until now. But his eyes . . . his song . . . it has to be him.

Jude. He said his name was Jude.

How did he survive that leap off the cliff? How on earth did he get inside the Convent? And how in all the universe of possibilities is he playing here now, for her? How did he become the one?

But he's wild! Nora thinks. *This is wrong. He shouldn't be here. This is dangerous. Don't be reckless. I have to tell the mothers . . .*

But she knows she can't tell them. Not yet. She's helpless to resist the force inside her. She doesn't even want to resist it.

I will choose him.

She knows it even before the tall, handsome, and otherwise perfectly good cello suitor plays. But the performance confirms her decision. The tall suitor attempts to copy the Trill but falters after only a few notes. It persists courageously but continues to miss notes, to backtrack, to repeat. The Trill's notes come too fast and too foreign for anyone to copy in one try. Even Nora took an entire day to learn it.

The music stops. The Hall falls silent.

Nora steps forward, between the two suitors. She looks to the tall suitor and smiles warmly. The suitor grins back but with little of its former confidence.

You will be a fine citizen, she tries to say with her eyes.

She turns to the wild boy. Jude.

His intense eyes overflow with energy, sending a current of excitement through her. She reaches out and takes his hand. Their touch is electric. Their arms raise into the air.

The crowd lets out a sound unlike any heard in the Hall before. It is lively and excited. It is almost wild.

19

♂

Courting

JUDE STANDS IN SHOCK, AMAZED at his own victory. The real live girl—the one who'd worn the red dress, the one who'd proved dreams come true—she took his hand. She chose him.

Her touch sends a pulsing power through his body, like a herd of galloping horses. People are cheering. The girl is moving down the aisle, taking him with her along the red carpet, between the pews of onlookers.

Riding the stampede of emotions he manages to follow her out of the vast sanctuary, guided by two older women in white robes. No one says a word.

They pass through a series of corridors until they reach one that looks very different. There's no red carpet. It is a bare gray hall lined with metal doors. Each door has a number.

The two white-robed women stop before an open door.

"This will be the sire's quarters," one of them says to the girl, as if Jude doesn't exist. "You may grow acquainted tonight. Write down any notes for us on the paper inside. There will be further testing tomorrow, and a potential first harvest."

The girl bows. "Thank you, mother."

She guides Jude into a large room. The door closes behind them. They're alone.

When Jude meets the girl's eyes, she quickly looks away as if taking in the surroundings. The smooth floor is warmed by a lush red carpet with florets of gold and amber. Paintings of fruit hang on the hard gray walls. A fire crackles in the hearth and a hundred candles glow. The back wall of the room is . . . missing.

"Go to the window," the girl says. "You'll like the view."

Window? Jude thinks. A window is a small square hole in his family's cabin. This room has no such thing. The back of the room is wide open, with the darkness of night outside. He moves toward it and discovers glass.

"It opens. Watch." The girl presses something on the wall by the door and the glass lifts like a curtain.

Jude gazes over the edge and breathes out, "Wow."

The floor hangs suspended on a cliff, high above a river. To the right a waterfall roars and sprays white foam below. Mist grazes Jude's cheek.

This can't be real.

The girl comes close to his side. Her presence suddenly makes the room and the waterfall irrelevant.

"What do you think?" she asks.

He can't take his eyes off her. "Amazing."

She smiles and turns away. "Come, let's sit and talk."

She moves to a red velvet chair in front of the fire and motions for him to take the seat opposite hers.

He lowers himself onto the chair, within reach of her.

"You played well," she says.

"Thanks. You too."

"That last song, the Devil's Trill. How did you learn it?"

"Lots of practice."

"With Ma? She taught your brother, too."

Her words hit him like a slap in the face. He's suddenly alert. Her beauty and the room's soft luster had dulled his senses. This is still enemy territory.

"How do you know that?" he asks.

"So you're really his brother."

She's the one who captured Esau. He told them about me.

Jude speaks carefully. "Why do you think I have a brother?"

"You didn't deny it. Surely you remember. We saw each other in the wild. Once by the river. Again by the cliff, after we caught your brother. You haven't forgotten that, have you?"

No, I never will. "I am a citizen here."

"You're not a very good liar. But it took me a while to realize it, with your dark curly hair shaved off. You played the Devil's Trill just like your brother. He's at rest now."

At rest. That's what the boy in the barn said. "What did you do to him?"

"The same thing we do with all our captives." She leans

forward in her chair. Her hand goes to his knee. "Except for you. I chose you. You could become a sire."

Jude stares at her and feels two tsunamis swelling inside, giant waves from opposite ends of the sea that are destined to collide. The first wave is wonder and desire. If not for this place and its evil, she could be his real live dream girl. Their duet, their touch, is nothing like a practiced piece on the violin. It's wild and reckless and electric. Even now, knowing what he knows, Jude wonders at her power over him.

But the second wave is panic and fear. This room with its niceties and smells does not change what Jude has seen and heard. The boys here are neutered slaves. They act like they *want* to be slaves. They're not even boys anymore. And the *wild* ones are put to rest.

Further testing, the older woman said. *A potential harvest.*

He's their prisoner.

And they're the ones who took Pa and Esau and Ma. They burned his home. They took everything from him. No matter how much he likes this girl, he knows he has to fight this place, even to destroy it if he can.

But how can he do that from inside? The Convent is too strong. There are too many of them.

"I take your silence as confirmation," the girl says. "You're the boy I saw in the wild. And you somehow snuck in here and dazzled us—dazzled me—with your performance. Tell me, how did you get here?"

The panic wave surges higher. She seems to know everything. Were they watching him all along?

"I don't know what you're talking about," he says.

"Let's try a different angle. *Why* did you come here?" She puts a finger to his chest. "What do *you* want?"

The girl's simple questions surf over his waves of desire and panic, crashing over him.

What do I want? Revenge! And you! And freedom!

A rational part of him, a tiny boat barely afloat among these waves, tells him to get leverage. He can't just play the notes on the page. He has to find a different way.

"So?" the girl asks, studying him curiously.

Jude feels sucked in by her amber eyes. He sees in them an answer she would like. He realizes in a way it's the same thing he wants. He needs to lower her guard.

His voice softens. "I want beauty."

"Like the beautiful sound we made together?"

"That was a start."

She lets out a little laugh and it tosses his little boat on the waves. She stands and holds out her hand.

He can't think. He needs to think.

"Come, I want to show you something else."

Jude eyes her pale, slender hand. He remembers something Pa once said. When a storm is everywhere around you, don't fight it. Ride it out.

He reaches out and takes her hand. Her energy carries him to the ledge suspended over the river.

A gust of cold wind blows over them. It parts the clouds in Jude's mind. He glimpses a way out. Yes. It could work. He should do it. They took everything from him. Now he will take from them. An eye for an eye.

The girl points up at the night sky. "See that constellation? Orion's belt?"

He nods. He sees it. She still has his hand. She's so close he can smell her. Lavender and rose. His heart pounds as he thinks of what he's about to do.

"Orion is a warrior," she says. "We don't need his kind anymore. But I'll admit I've wondered what he'd be like here. I think maybe he'd be like you."

She squeezes his hand, nearly sinks his boat. The sound of the waterfall is the only thing buoying him up. The water has pounded down for ages, deepening the pool, softening the landing. He still has the element of surprise.

"Maybe," he says, leaning closer to the edge and pointing at the waterfall. The cooler air steadies his nerves. Time to take the initiative. "If I'm Orion, then does that make you Venus?"

"Who's that?"

Her response puzzles Jude. How can she know about Orion and not Venus? He says, "A mythical goddess who emerged from the ocean. That's where this river leads."

"I don't understand."

"I will teach you." He smiles and steps closer to her. "Venus came from the ocean. Maybe she should go back. That's where this water goes."

She looks profoundly confused. "What do you mean?"

"This." He grips her hand tight, pulls her close.

Then, in a motion so sudden and desperate that it allows

no resistance, he leaps off the ledge and into the waterfall's spray, taking the girl with him.

20

♀

Waterfall

NORA FLIES INTO THE DARKNESS without form and void. The sire's room vanished. There was the warm fire and the soft carpet under her feet. Now there's only the bare night, without the ground to steady it. The only fixed point is the boy's vice grip on her hand, even as their arms and legs start to flail.

Gravity doesn't delay long.

They plummet. Wind whips Nora's hair. The waterfall roars and sprays blinding mist. She hears a high and violent F sharp note. It's her scream.

Water rushes up and hits her like a cold punch to the face.

She sinks deep under the river, under the pounding of the waterfall. She opens her eyes frantically and sees nothing. It's pitch black. Shock freezes her body.

How sad, she thinks, *to die underwater.*

But then she's yanked up. The boy pulls her hand and her head pops above the churning, frothy surface. The current races away with her body, further from the waterfall. She hits a rock, hard. Her shoulder cries in pain. The boy's hand still holds hers.

The rapids spit them out into a quieter pool. The river widens. Nora treads as best she can, but it's far to either shore.

The boy wraps his arm around her chest and leans back and swims, hauling her with him. His feet kick steadily. His one free arm pulls hard with each stroke. His breathing is heavy by her ear. He's stronger than he looked.

Nora's feet finally touch bottom. They crawl out of the water onto a rocky bank, near a large willow that dips into the shallows. Large boulders enclose the area, with forest beyond.

Nora drops down onto her back and stares up. She sees Orion's Belt. Her chest heaves up and down, trying to make sense of what happened. She puts her hand to her neck. The emerald necklace is not there. Her fist clenches.

No. Mother God, no.

At least she's alive. She can't believe she survived the fall. It was all too fast. She hurts, inside and out. Her shoulder throbs. Her heart aches.

She hears the boy doing something nearby. He gathers sticks among the scattered rocks, then forms a small stack in front of her. She glimpses a spark. Moments later a fire grows.

The boy comes closer, and she recoils away.

He wraps a blanket around her.

Teeth chattering, he says, "Must warm up." He curls shivering into the blanket beside her, before the flames.

She cringes at his closeness, but warmth spreads slowly

through her. With the heat comes anger, a blaze of fury.

How dare this boy?

He broke every rule. He snuck into the Convent. He pretended to be a citizen. Then he took her away from everything she knows, without warning and against her will. It's savage. It's terrible. It proves the Convent's wisdom. These male beasts must be eliminated or tamed. And now he tries to be close to her, to warm her, to comfort her?

How dare he?

"You okay?" he asks.

No! Nora wants to scream. She could tell him that whatever he's trying to do, it will fail. They'll come for her. The mothers will track them wherever he tries to take her, wherever he goes. But it's better to give him no warning.

She grits her teeth and looks away.

"I don't want to hurt you," he says. "I'll take care of you. What do you need?"

Her eyes flick toward him. He wears a smug little grin, lit by the crackling flames. No matter how gentle he appears, he will pay for what he's done. She closes her eyes and turns away.

"Okay, I'll let you sleep," he says.

He lies down, curling up by her side.

She holds still and pretends to sleep. The mothers won't discover she's gone until morning. She can't wait that long. She can't be far from the Convent.

As soon as his breathing deepens, she'll run.

21

♂

Hot Chocolate

JUDE LIES STILL AND STUDIES the flames and listens to Nora breathe. She's like ice. She refuses to talk to him, not that he's not surprised. He lassoed the sun and yanked her down a waterfall. He took her from her home. He knows how that feels, even if her home is a twisted lie.

I'll win her over, he thinks. *I just need time.*

They should have until morning before the Convent will discover they're gone. *You may grow acquainted tonight, more testing tomorrow*, the old woman said before she left them alone in the well-decorated prison cell. She didn't expect their "acquaintance" to involve a swim and an open fire under the stars. Jude knows they need to get further away from the Convent before dawn, but they had to warm up. It will be slow going if the girl resists.

Jude smiles to himself, amazed that he got out alive with her. He scoots closer under the blanket. She doesn't budge.

"You asleep?" he whispers.

No response. Her breathing is steady.

She could be faking sleep, Jude knows. She could try to run. He uses that as his excuse for putting a hand on her shoulder, softly. If she stirs, he'll notice.

Weariness wraps around him, nestled under the blanket, close to the sun. There's nothing like diving off a waterfall into a frigid river, then sitting by a warm crackling fire, to make the eyes heavy. Better than a lullaby, other than one by Ma.

Thanks to Ma, Jude had prepared for something like this. He found his things right where he'd left them—in a hidden cove under a willow, tucked into his family's canoe, *The Odyssey*. They'd freeze to death without the fire and blanket. He'd managed to find enough wood around the rocks, probably left by river floods. Now he and the girl are warm, together, quiet. They have enough food for a couple days.

Jude starts to drift off. A lucid dream of the girl playing the violin sweeps him gently toward sleep.

Then she sighs. The faint, sweet sound pulls Jude back. Her breathing has deepened. It is regular, in and out. Another sigh, almost a laugh. She must be dreaming.

He draws closer. Her warmth and smell cast a spell over his thawing body. He falls asleep, curled beside her.

He wakes with a start.

A rooster crows in the distance.

Nora still sleeps, but the fire has burned down to coals. Jude eyes the dark, starless sky and listens. The stillness of night gives way to the song of birds. Another faint rooster

119

crow signals first light coming soon. He didn't mean to sleep so long. He's not used to having another warm body beside his.

They need to move fast, to put as much distance between them and the Convent as possible. Reluctantly, he slips away from her and moves to his bag in the canoe. In it he finds his metal cup and a treat he'd been saving for a special occasion: a single piece of chocolate. He does as Ma taught him and sets the chocolate in the cup, fills it with water, and places it by the coals to warm. He moves quickly with other preparations to cast off into the river.

Soon the fragrance drifts from the fire. The first pale light creeps into the horizon. The girl stirs.

He takes the cup to her. "Morning treat."

She sits up with a start. "Poison?"

"Much better. Trust me. It'll warm you up."

"You drink it first."

Jude grins at her obstinance as she sits curled and looking forlorn in the blanket. He takes a sip and savors the taste, the moment. He offers it to her again.

She still hesitates, fixing him with an uncertain glare.

His eyes meet hers, steady and full of warmth. "I think you will like it."

She takes the cup and sips and her glare slowly softens. She yawns and rubs her eyes. Color returns to her cheeks in the light of the early morning and the dying coals. She glows like an angel.

"What you did . . . it's insane," she says. "Why?"

"That room was too stuffy."

"So you threw me into a waterfall?"

"We jumped together. It would be no good being out here alone, without you. Your people took everything I had."

"We didn't take anything."

"I saw it happen. They kidnapped my brother Esau at night, by the lake. Then a woman came to our home. She killed our dog. Then . . . I heard the gunshot and . . . she killed Ma . . ." Jude chokes up but manages to add: "Burned it all."

"That can't be true. We don't resort to violence. The Convent is a place of love and beauty. You saw that in the Great Hall. Your brother Esau is fine."

The lie shocks him. "No violence? I saw your people take down Esau."

"With gas. It was harmless."

"How do *you* know that?"

"I was there."

"You . . ." Jude remembers the figures in the night. The masks and the gas. His real live girl is dangerous. "*You* started this."

She sips the hot chocolate. "Your brother was trespassing."

"So you gassed him and put him to rest? You *killed* him!"

"No, no, no. I said he was *at* rest now. He's doing much better, now that his trouble is gone."

Jude's knees go weak. "Wait. He's alive?"

"Of course he is. I told you, we are peaceful. We are trying to help him. We can go back and I will take you to him."

"What have you done to him?"

"We played music together. He's good, though not quite as talented as you. We should go back. Your gifts will be praised at the Convent. I told you. We live in peace."

He doesn't believe her. It can't be that simple. He takes a step back, closer to the river, to escape. "Did you come to our home, too?"

"No. When did that happen?"

"A couple days ago."

The girl looks down into the cup, as if puzzling over something. "Did you actually see anyone hurt?"

"They killed our dog."

"That's it, then. Animals are different. Maybe it was decided to extend tender mercy to your dog rather than leave it alone as your mother joined the Convent."

"*Mercy?* Ma would never join the Convent. They shot her!"

"No, we wouldn't hurt her. It's not our way. It sounds like your family is in the Convent, so all you had to do was stay to see them. I *chose* you."

She sounds as if she was betrayed. He still doesn't trust her, but she's given him new hope. Maybe Esau really is alive. What if Ma is, too? Maybe even Pa? Still, he can't just go back now. Not yet. He has the girl. He has to figure out how to use her as leverage.

"They'll come searching for you," he says.

She doesn't reply. They fall into silence.

Jude takes a deep breath of the fresh predawn air. Silver

ripples bend around a boulder in the river. There's a sudden splash—a fish nipping a bug off the surface. This is why he had to leave. The Convent's lies are weaker out here. Only the truth can withstand the relentless force of nature.

Jude gathers the empty cup and the blanket. "Time to go."

She crosses her arms. "I'm not going anywhere with you."

Jude expected this. Faint chance hot chocolate would convince her. The Convent is only a short hike away. More light grays the sky. The longer she stalls the more risk they'll be caught.

He has one option left: threat. He goes to his bag and draws the shotgun hidden there. He checks the safety. It's on. It's unloaded, too.

He turns and aims at her.

"Get up," he says as firmly as he can.

She rises to her feet, eyes wide as a doe. He's suddenly aware of her body. She's tall. Lean muscles show under her silky white dress. Her chest heaves with adrenalin.

"You won't shoot," she says.

Jude doesn't argue. "I'll make you go one way or another."

"Oh? A strong boy like you?" Her face broadens into a sultry smile. She takes a step closer. "Why don't we stay here and keep each other warm?"

She reaches out and delicately touches the gun's barrel.

Jude feels confused, almost dizzy. He lets the gun lower and steps back.

Then she strikes. Her punch hits him in the gut. He bends over just as her knee jerks up and slams between his legs.

He crumples to the ground, still clutching the gun.

She stomps on his hand, knocks the gun loose.

No, he gasps in pain, panics.

She kicks at his head.

He rolls away and deflects her foot and manages to clasp her ankle. With a quick yank he sweeps her off balance. He surges to his feet as she goes down hard. He grabs the gun and spins, tense and ready to defend against the next assault.

But it doesn't come. She lies still.

He kneels carefully beside her. There's a large rock by her head. She must have landed on it. He puts his hand gently to her neck. She has a pulse. She's breathing, but knocked out cold.

"Dear Lord," he whispers. "Let her live."

This is *not* what he wanted. Ma would skin him. But that will have to wait.

He drags Nora to the canoe and lays her as comfortably as he can in the curved hull. He quickly shoves off. The river carries them downstream, away from the Convent and into the wild.

22

♀

Odyssey

THE WORLD WOBBLES as consciousness blooms in Nora. She lies on her back, nestled under a blanket and pressed tight on both sides. The blue sky is so bright it hurts her head. Trees frame the edges of her vision. She hears a soft current of water.

She remembers: the waterfall, the boy, the fight.

Her plan almost worked. She lulled him off guard, then struck. He fought back like the dangerous species that he is. And he had the gun. At least he didn't shoot it. But he tripped her, and then she hit the ground and everything went black.

She winces as she slowly sits up, rocking back and forth. The pain is everywhere—bruised shoulder, aching limbs, pounding temple. They're in a small canoe near the edge of the river. The boy sits in front of her, within reach, gazing ahead and paddling steadily.

The shore is not too far. If she could flip them and . . .

The boy turns back to her. His knuckles are white against

the paddle's dark wood. He looks tired. "Glad you're up. You okay?"

She shakes her head and rubs her throbbing temple, where there's a scabbed lump. A question scratches out of her parched lips. "How long?"

"There was evening and there was morning, the first day. Let there be waters, the second day."

His strange words make her head hurt worse. She asks, "It's been a whole day and night?"

"Yes, a new beginning." The boy pats the rim of the boat fondly. "The Odyssey rocked you like a baby as you slept."

"Odyssey?"

"That's the name of my mighty boat. *Our* mighty boat."

He glances ahead. With two brisk strokes he steers the canoe around a small boulder jutting up from the river's surface.

The river is wide here. Water flows in slow, uneventful currents. The sun is halfway up the horizon, and from the chill in the air and the directions of the shadows, she knows it's morning. She can't believe she was out for so long. Even at this slow pace, they must be miles from the Convent.

She stretches her arms and breathes deep of the cold air and thinks. The mothers will send help. By now they know she's missing. They won't find any tracks, so they'll figure out that the boy took her by river. She will be rescued.

But how long will it be? She wonders. *Run or wait?*

"You hungry?" the boy asks. "Thirsty?"

She shakes her head.

"Well, let me know if you need anything."

She glares at him, with a scowl unlike any she's ever worn. How dare he pretend to be nice after what he did?

He shrugs and turns back to paddling.

Her fingers dip into the water by the canoe's side. The little ripples shine like silver. It looks shallow enough to stand. She cups her hand and lifts water to her mouth. It tastes cold and refreshing. She drinks more, getting a feel for the water and a plan.

She has to slow the boy down. And she's never liked waiting.

In one swift motion she surges up and dives into the river.

The frigid water is painful medicine. She forgets the headache and ignores that her feet don't quite touch the bottom. She swims as hard as she can for the shore.

There's a splash behind her. The boy's coming.

She doesn't look back. She goes faster.

It takes only a few more strokes before her feet find the silty bottom. She rushes ahead to the shore, then she takes off running. Her head throbs with each step. Her soaked dress clings to her. But her lungs burn for freedom.

At the top of the riverbank she risks a glance back. The boy has dragged the boat to the shore. Now he's gaining on her. She can't outrun him.

Ahead there's a rocky outcrop—high ground. She forges through underbrush and scrambles up the side of boulders. She lifts herself onto the largest stone. Atop it, above all the surroundings, she rests with her hands on her knees, panting and watching the boy come.

In moments he climbs up after her. He reaches to hoist himself onto her boulder. She stomps his fingers.

He yelps and stands back. He looks very small beneath her. Between heavy breaths he says, "You can't stay up there forever."

Nora grabs a fist-sized rock and hurls it at him. He dodges it easily, but stays back. Every moment of delay is a victory.

"They'll come for me," she says.

"I'm planning on that."

"What's your plan? To hold me hostage?"

"I'm planning to take you back to the boat and keep going down the river."

"And then what?"

"There's a safe place we can rest."

Nora doesn't believe him. "And then what?"

The boy looks up as a robin swoops overhead, singing. "See, the birds have it figured out," he says. "Do not worry about tomorrow. Today has enough trouble of its own. So come on down."

She shakes her head. This boy is a fool. Help will come for her.

"Are you just going wait there like king of the hill?" he asks.

"Queen."

The boy laughs. It makes Nora furious. She grabs another rock and throws and barely misses.

"I'm taking you with me," the boy says.

"Good luck."

"I don't want to hurt you."

Nora's hand moves to her temple. "You already did."

"It was an accident, and you started it. I never meant for you to get hurt. Come down and I promise it won't happen again."

"I don't trust you."

"Figures. Ma says women never trust men."

"You're only a boy."

He smiles wide as the river. "And you're my girl."

She hurls another rock and this time connects, striking his shoulder so hard he cries out in pain.

"That's it," he mutters. He turns away and retreats.

Nora raises a fist in quiet conquest. A feeling creeps up from deep within and it surprises her: pride. She didn't realize how much she wanted to prevail over this boy at his own game. It distracted her from the most important thing. Getting back home.

She starts to shout for help, as loud as she can, over and over. "*Help, help, help!*" The word echoes through the forest, over ridges, through valleys, up the river. Let it shine like a beacon. If anyone is near, they will come.

But there is no answer. The boy returns with a pack at his back. He circles the boulder, moving warily as if sizing her up.

Nora doesn't feel good about this. She stops shouting and swivels as he moves, always keeping her eyes locked on him. She readies herself for the gun, but he doesn't seem to have it. Maybe he left it in the canoe. The river could have damaged it. He wouldn't have risked drenching it in the swim.

She breathes easier. Then she throws another rock and misses.

The next rock is smaller but hits him in the leg. He stumbles and bends down and moans, but then he goes back to circling. He suddenly stops and pulls out a rope.

Before she realizes what he's doing, he slings the rope up. She raises her arms to beat it away, but a loop falls over her wrist and immediately cinches tight.

The boy yanks her forward. Her footing slips as she goes over the edge. She flails as she falls.

The boy rushes forward with his arms out.

Her body hits his like an avalanche. They both fall hard to the ground. All the air is knocked from her lungs.

The boy struggles up and, before she can budge, ties her wrists together like he's a cowboy binding a runaway calf. Then he coils the rope around to bind her arms tight against her sides. She twists and tries to run, but he jerks the rope and yanks her down. She glares up at him.

He gives the rope a tug. "On your feet," he grunts. "Walk."

"Make me," Nora says.

"I'll drag you if I have to."

"You said you wouldn't hurt me."

"*If* you came down. This is not the way I want it."

He sounds so sincere, so frustrated, that she almost believes him. *No, not after what he did. His kind can't be trusted.*

Still, she can't run or fight or do much of anything while she's tied up, so she rises furiously and defiantly to her feet. He turns and leads her back toward the river by the rope.

She needs to slow them down. She needs the Convent to find her. She screams again, "*Help!*"

The boy yanks her to the ground. The woods respond to her shouts with silence.

"No more of that," he says. "Please, just walk."

She rises, thinking furiously of her options. She sees the river through the trees. It's close. With a head start, she could get to the canoe first. She could paddle faster than he swims.

She forces herself to smile and steps toward the boy. "Thanks for saying please. If you will *please* untie the rope, I'll go."

He studies her, looking unsure. "Fine, but if you run or shout, I'll have to tie you up again. Got it?"

She nods. He approaches warily and unties the rope. Stepping back, he coils it to put it in his bag.

It's halfway in, his arms wrestling with it, when she charges and shoves him back. He falls and she runs.

It's fast down the hill, dodging trees, leaping roots. He's coming now. She's almost there, a stone's throw. She glances back to make sure she'll beat him. It's a good lead. But her right foot lands wrong and catches a root. Her ankle twists and pops. She goes down hard.

She grunts and tries to rise. Her ankle gives under the weight, flooding with pain. She falls back again.

The boy rushes to her and kneels close. He gently lifts her

leg and slides off her shoe. She bites her lip and hurts too much to resist. His fingers prod on her skin, where it already swells and turns pinkish purple. "Looks like a bad sprain. We need to get this elevated."

"It's all your fault," she says, trying not to cry.

"I warned you. Can you stand?" He holds his hand out to her. "Here, you can lean on me as we go."

She considers spitting on it. "I don't want to go."

He pulls a leaf out of her hair. "That's not an option. We're going together, and we can do it the easy way or the hard way."

The hard way. She swats his hand away, but she knows she's lost this battle. The mothers are absolutely right about these creatures. The boy started a war, and it is a war she and the Convent will win. He will be tamed, whatever it takes. But she needs to rest, to prepare for the next battle. She takes his hand.

He pulls her up and slides her arm over his shoulder, bracing her. She hops on her one good foot as they make their way to the river. It's hard to navigate through the trees, hobbling beside him. She feels tired and woozy. She slips a couple times, but he keeps her steady.

They reach the canoe on the silty shore. He helps her climb aboard. He arranges his bag so that she can lean back and prop up her ankle.

"Comfortable?" he asks.

"No. It hurts."

"I'm sorry. It's the best I can do. You need rest."

She looks away. A spider skates along the smooth water. A fish jumps from the surface. She lies helpless.

He pushes out into the river and paddles ahead. "Let me know if you get hungry," he says. "I'll catch something."

She glares at him. *This is not over. This is only the beginning.*

23

♂

Fishing

THE FISHING LINE CUTS a slender path through the languid water. It's midday and cool and Jude knows this is the worst time to catch anything. He has little choice. They need food. It's been four days since they leapt from the Convent.

The girl has barely talked after her last attempted escape. Jude learned his mistake: he should have tied her up in the boat. She will not come without a fight, no matter how much kindness or hot chocolate he offers. Even after she hurt her ankle and had no chance of running away, she tried yelling out. The sound carried over the river, a terrible siren call. He had to tie a cloth over her mouth.

The next day he'd seen familiar landmarks along the river—a tree hanging over a bend, a rock in the shape of a face. His former home was close. He felt sure the Convent would have people waiting there, expecting him. If they found him now, they'd capture him and take the girl and make all this count for nothing. He needs the girl hidden when he talks to the women. That's the only way he'd have leverage to trade her for Esau or his parents, if they're still alive.

So he couldn't trust the girl, even with a cloth over her mouth. He had stopped the canoe far enough upstream, out of earshot he hoped, and waited until night. The girl tired out and fell asleep.

He paddled swiftly under the stars, on the far side of the river, obscured by mist from the other shore. They passed the burnt remains of his home without trouble. He cried only a little, silently.

Morning came and still she slept. When she woke, he told her he was sorry he had no food to offer. He took off the cloth so she could drink some water. Then she went to sleep again.

Now he's still paddling, dragging the fishing line behind and trying to ignore the grumbles of his empty stomach and the blisters on his hands. They should reach the island by evening. His family always kept backup supplies there. It won't solve everything, but it should be a safe place to shelter and decide what to do next.

He glances back at Nora. She almost seems to have accepted her fate. Her chest rises and falls steadily under her dress. The fine white fabric is torn and dirty, but her face is serene and flawless. She's beautiful when she sleeps. Jude wonders what she dreams. Probably not about him.

It didn't have to be this way, he thinks.

His paddling continues in rhythm. Left side, right side, left, right, smooth and steady as the canoe glides along. An hour passes. He yawns and dozes off.

The fishing line goes tight.

It pulls so fast and heavy that the canoe almost tips over. The girl sits up and watches him. He braces himself to haul in the catch. As he drags the line, the fish pulls back, tugging the canoe toward shore. It's strong but slower than any fish he's ever caught.

Patiently, Jude coils the line around the crossbeam of the canoe after each pull. The fish's fight fades. The gap closes.

At last the river surface breaks. Jude grunts in surprise.

It's a giant snapper. The turtle's beady eyes and snout flare like an angry, ancient dinosaur.

Jude considers cutting the line. One snap from the creature's beak could take a finger.

No. Can't give up. We need food.

He remembers something Pa used to say, "Turtle soup's gotten me through many a cold day." Pa also had a big scar on his hand where a snapper once clamped down with its mighty jaws. "My own Ma punched it off," Pa said with a rare grin.

Soup without a scar, that's the goal, Jude decides. Ahead he sees the river fork around a small island. It's the one. He paddled faster than he thought.

He'll have a better chance if the canoe is stable. Dragging the snapper behind, he guides the canoe to the silty shore at the head of the island.

"New pet?" the girl asks.

Jude blinks in surprise. She took off the cloth over her mouth. But she isn't shouting, so he lets it be.

"Dinner," he says.

Her face twists in disgust but she doesn't say more.

The canoe bumps to a stop. Jude hops out with the fishing line in hand. He circles around the canoe warily. The turtle's front legs and claws grip a small log by the shore. Its eyes lock onto Jude like the enemy he is. The hook in its mouth dangles like a villain's cigarette.

Jude squares off with the primordial creature. He crouches and moves forward with his razor blade in hand. He gets close and slices down. The turtle snaps and nearly clamps his hand. Another inch and he'd have four fingers.

"My bet's on the turtle." The girl sounds amused.

Resolve surges up in Jude. He steps to the canoe and pulls out his gun. The metal barrel locks onto the ancient dinosaur. Praying it still works, he pulls the trigger.

Boom.

Birds caw and soar away. The river goes quiet as death.

"That was messy," the girl says.

Jude nods, lowering the gun. "And now it's dinner."

24

♀

Shelter

THE TURTLE STARTS TO SMELL in the late afternoon. It's not the smell of decay, but of raw meat and blood. Flesh and iron. Nora tries to keep her eyes away from the dead creature. She prays for a fresh breeze. But the river is still and quiet as the sun lowers to the treetops, where leaves catch the light like golden nets.

After shooting the turtle, the boy helped her out of the canoe, tied her to a tree with wrists bound behind her back, and left her. He said he needed to scout the island and would be back soon. It's been at least an hour. The island didn't look that big.

She studies the ropes for the hundredth time. The boy knows how to tie a knot, she'll give him that. She's tried to wriggle free, to do anything to get out of her bind, but she's gotten nothing but chafed skin on her wrists. Not that she'd make it far if she got loose, with her ankle swollen like a cantaloupe. At the Convent they'd treat her with a splint and a healing salve. Her muscles feel tighter than the ropes, hunched as she's been in the canoe. Help will come, she assures herself. The Convent will find her. The mothers will not give up.

She hears a rustle of leaves. The boy approaches through the forest. His ruddy face shines in the day's last light. When he comes closer, she smells him more than the turtle. He brings a pungent mix of leather and sweat, with an odd hint of apricot.

"I found it," he says. "Not as much food as I'd hoped, but a little. And good shelter."

"A house?" Nora asks.

"A cave. I'll carry you."

"I can walk."

He looks down at her ankle. "Come on, let me help."

"Fine."

He unties the rope where it connects to the tree, but he leaves the knot binding her wrists behind her back. With a grunt he lifts her.

"Light as a feather," he says with a grin.

Nora frowns up at him as he carries her away. His arms are stronger than they look.

The boy carries her through thick underbrush. Briars fill the space between the trees like a thorny swamp. One of them catches Nora's cheek as they pass, and she lets out a yelp.

"Sorry," the boy says.

He turns and wades through the briars backwards. Nora receives not another scratch.

They ascend a hillside. At the top there's a rocky outcrop. From there she can see the entire island, jutting up from the middle of the broad river. Downstream the gentle water stretches for miles before it curves around a bend.

The boy approaches a large boulder and turns sideways to slip into an opening barely wide enough for the two of them. Inside there's a small cave only a few paces wide. It's dark and damp and cold. The boy sets Nora down on the hard stone ground.

"Don't go anywhere," he says. "I'll be back."

"I'll miss you," she says, deadpan.

"Miss you, too!" His cheery smile infuriates her.

Left tied up and alone again, she studies the inside of the cave. It's more of a hole between rocks. The back wall has a natural rock shelf, where a black box, a pot, and a few large glass jars are lined up. The jars have labels with orderly script: *beans, tomatoes, peaches*. There are smaller jars, too, without labels but with familiar-looking contents. Salt, pepper, coffee, corn meal, and maybe sugar.

It makes her empty stomach growl, but it makes her heart sick. The boy could keep her captive here for weeks, maybe months.

Stay calm, she tells herself. *Think like a mother*.

Fighting didn't work, and she feels a little guilty for even trying it. That's the way of men, the way of evil. Running didn't work, either. It left her worse off. Shouting only gave her a sore throat. They are too far from the Convent for anyone to hear.

She needs to gain control of the boy with her words. She needs to convince him to do what she wants to do. But first, she needs the blasted scratchy ropes off her wrists.

She scoots to a stone jutting up from the floor and feels its edge. It's no knife, but it might do the job. She drags the rope against the stone. She feels friction but there's no cut. She puts all her weight into it, leaning over the stone and grinding the rope backward and forward.

In a brief rest from the effort, she hears the boy approaching. She sits back and puts on an innocent face.

He enters with his bag slung over his back and the dead turtle in his arms. He sets them down in the corner. With only a passing glance at her, he turns to go again.

The smell of the turtle overwhelms the little cave. She goes to work again on the rope. This time the boy returns much sooner, with a bundle of sticks in his arms. They're as skinny and knobby as his legs.

"I could help," Nora says.

He stops and studies her. "You think I'm stupid?"

"Why would you think that?"

He shakes his head. "You'd run."

She motions to her ankle. "I can't run."

"Then you'd crawl. You'd find the canoe and flee by river. Or worse, you'd take my gun and . . . well, after what happened last time, let's just say you'll have to earn my trust."

Off he goes again.

Maybe he's not stupid, Nora has to admit. He's managed to drag her away from the Convent without getting caught.

She returns to the sharp stone and the rope, pausing whenever the boy returns with more sticks.

After his fourth or fifth trip, she finally wears through the rope, setting her wrists free. She rises slowly and stretches her arms overhead, bending forward and back. She sighs in quiet satisfaction. She's been hunched over for days.

The boy returns again. Nora quickly arranges her rope so that it still looks tied behind her. The boy stacks leaves and dry sticks at the center of the cave, then lights it with a match from his pack. He whistles an unfamiliar tune as he works.

Soon a fire burns and a pot of water boils. The boy sets to cutting turtle meat and dropping it into the pot. He sprinkles salt and spices on top.

Smells good, Nora admits. Her mouth waters.

The boy dips a spoon into the pot and tastes it. He smiles.

Then he fills a first bowl and offers it to her. Nora hesitates. She has to move carefully, to hide the rope she cut.

"Go on," the boy says. "I know you're untied."

Nora's mouth falls open. She starts to defend herself, but he continues.

"And I know you're hungry. It's not bad. Try it."

Nora accepts the bowl with her hands cupped together. She takes a sip. Warmth fills her and she lets out a small, contented sigh.

"Not bad, eh?"

"It's good," she says. "How did you learn to cook?"

"Ma taught me. She always let me hang around the kitchen and sneak a few bites. Eventually she put me to work.

Those were good times. Until your people came and killed her and burned our kitchen and house down."

Nora has been thinking about what the boy told her before. The timing troubles her, because it all happened around the same time that one of the mothers, Krystal, suddenly died in her sleep. She knows the mothers wouldn't lie, but she wonders if there was some kind of fight. It wouldn't quite be a lie if Krystal was shot and then died in her sleep. All the boy saw was the cabin burning.

"How many gunshots did you hear?" she asks.

"Just one. Why?"

"I think your Ma is still alive," she says. "The Convent wouldn't hurt her."

"I don't believe you."

"Do you know why we had the ceremony, when I picked you?"

He shrugs. "To pass the time?"

"I was selected to be the next mother." Nora struggles to keep the emotion out of her voice, remembering what she's lost. "There are twelve mothers, and one had died two nights before that. Her name was Krystal."

The boy puts down his bowl. "The woman who came to my cabin was named Krystal. She killed my dog. She shot Ma."

Nora shakes her head. "What if your Ma shot Krystal?"

"Ma would never. But." The boy's face brightens. "It's possible, I guess. Her life was in danger, so was mine. But the woman said there were others. There had to be, for the cabin to burn like that. Even if you're right, and boy, I sure hope you're right, wouldn't they kill Ma for killin' one of their own?"

"No, we are not violent. They would have brought her back to the Convent. Like we did with your brother."

"As a prisoner." The boy falls quiet, studying Nora. "If Ma and Esau are alive, would your people trade them for you?"

Trade? If that's the boy's plan, he has no chance. The mothers will not bargain with a kidnapper. But this could give her leverage.

"How would you communicate with them?" she asks.

"You said they'd come for you."

"Yes."

"Do you think they'll come this far?"

Yes, she thinks. "I doubt it."

"That's what I figured. We're a long way from your fence. But they'll have people at my old home, on watch. We'll go back there and I'll make the offer."

Nora feels a flicker of hope. "When?"

"Once your ankle is better."

"Then we'll go and meet them together."

He laughs. "Oh I'm sure you'd like that. As soon as they know where you are, they'll take you. I have another idea, but we need to get to the cabin together. Then, once they bring my family, if they're still alive, I'll let you go."

"You took me so I could be your pawn?"

"No. I mean, that's not why I took you. We were in that

room. With the fire and the warmth. And you were . . . you are . . . different."

Nora doesn't know what to say. He went from laughing to emotional in an instant, and his words don't make sense. Of course she's different, certainly from him, a boy with T inside. She decides to change the subject, to lower his guard. "What was the song you were whistling earlier?"

"An old folk song," he says.

"Who wrote it?"

"No one particular."

"How is that possible?"

"It grew out of life. Music works that way."

"Music gives life meaning."

He smiles. "No, life gives music meaning."

Nora takes another sip of soup. She doesn't want to argue. "Who's your favorite composer?" she asks.

"Tchaikovsky."

Nora blinks in surprise. How can they have the same favorite? "Why him?"

"He balances power and delicacy better than anyone. Who's yours?"

"The same."

"Oh."

They finish the soup in quiet, with their awkward agreement lingering like a temporary truce in the little cave. The fire crackles and gives light as darkness falls outside.

Nora hands her bowl back. "Thanks for the soup. You were right about the turtle."

"You're welcome." The boy looks at her wrists. "Do I need to tie you up tonight?"

Nora puts on her best smile, partly sincere. "I can't run on my ankle, and where would I go? We're on an island."

"And I hid the canoe," the boy says.

"I'll stay tonight. I promise."

"Fool me twice, shame on me. Fool me thrice, you won't get another chance. Understood?"

Nora nods, feeling the boy's eyes evaluating her.

"I like Antonio Vivaldi, too," she says. "He calms me down sometimes."

"You say that like you know him."

"We do! That's what I love most about music. We share it over time and space. We can feel what Vivaldi felt as if he were in this cave with us."

"I guess that's right," the boy says. "Well, I can't figure out how to say it, so . . ." He moves to the rock shelf on the wall and takes down the black box. He pulls out an old violin and tunes it by ear. He looks up at her. "This is how I feel."

He begins to play. It's Vivaldi and it's beautiful.

The rich sound and the firelight on the boy and the days of weariness and pain pile up and up into an emotion. Nora almost weeps but part of her resists. She won't let the boy bring her to that.

She just needs sleep. She'll figure out what to do tomorrow, if the mothers don't get here first. She rolls over and closes her eyes and lets the music wrap her in dreams.

25

♂

Bath

MORNING DAWNS CLEAR AND COOL. A perfect autumn day. Jude leaves Nora sleeping in the cave and makes his way to the southern tip of the island. The silty riverbank cushions his steps. The water glistens. He picks up a smooth stone and skips it as far as he can. He throws a dozen more, trying to shake loose his thoughts, to release his frustration. He lost his family, and now he could lose the girl.

He sits on the sand, elbows on his knees. On the far bank he sees a mother bear with two large cubs. They are catching trout, filling up to hibernate soon. He envies them. He wishes he and Nora could burrow into the little island cave and sleep through the winter. But they can't store up enough fat. Humans are wound up for ceaseless activity.

A bright yellow leaf falls to the water and drifts like a golden lily pad. A huge poplar tree hangs overhead. Jude remembers the deep pool under its branches. He and Esau came here in the summer and swung from a vine and dropped like rocks into the river. Those were fine days.

Will the Convent give up Esau? Is Ma alive?

He figures the only way he can find out is to go back to the cabin. He shudders at the memory of the flames as it burned. The women will be there. But they don't know about the tunnel from the riverbank, or the safe cellar room. He'll leave Nora here and tell the women that if they bring his family, they can have her back. But they could just take him and torture him until he tells where she is. It's a risk he'll have to take.

In the meantime, he'll learn as much as he can from Nora. Not that he trusts her, but she might reveal something about her people's strange way of thinking.

He trudges back up the hill.

When he reaches the cave, she's gone. Her footprints are detectable through the fallen leaves. The prints show normal walking strides, other than a shorter step that drags. She can't make it far on her ankle.

Jude follows after her trail. The steps lead north, to where he left the canoe. His stomach sinks. If she paddled off, there's no way he'll catch her. He can't lose her.

The footprints end at the riverbank within a stone's throw of the canoe. He glimpses it still in the hiding spot, under a fallen tree. At the shore there's a small pile of clothes.

Her head suddenly pops up from the river.

She has her back to him. She's taking a bath.

Jude feels his cheeks flush red. She won't be swimming away naked. She's also much bolder than he expected, dipping into this cold water.

He turns away to give her privacy, then finds a place on higher ground where he can keep an eye on the canoe. Only a minute or two passes before he sees her limping toward him. She looks like a nymph, her short hair dripping. Her dress still has tears, but it's wet and clean now. She washed it. She shivers with her hands clutching her elbows.

"Hi." Her teeth chatter loudly.

"Hi." Jude comes and puts her arm over his shoulder, supporting her. "You're freezing. Let's get to the fire."

He half carries her up the hill. Once she's in the cave, where coals are still warm, he quickly adds sticks and builds up the fire.

She leans close and holds her hands to the warmth.

He gives her a minute until her shivering calms, then he asks, "What were you thinking?"

"I was . . . filthy," she says through chatters.

"I thought you'd run away again."

"You said you're going to trade me."

"Yes."

"Then I might as well go with you."

Jude gazes at her in wonder. He wants to believe her. Maybe he really has earned some trust. He's fed her and kept her alive, after all.

"What do you think will happen?" he asks.

She hugs her blanket closer and stares at the fire. "They will be there at the cabin, like you said. When you tell them about your mother and brother, they will bring them and trade them for me."

"That simple?"

"I was chosen to be the next mother," she says, as if that answers everything.

"Can't any girl become a mother?"

"You don't understand."

"Then tell me, please."

She turns to him. Wrapped up, basked in firelight, and vulnerable, she looks more beautiful than ever. "We have perfect order at the Convent. There are twelve mothers who lead us. They give birth to new life. We live in peace and harmony. We create beauty."

"What about the other women? Can't they be mothers?"

"Only twelve," she says. "It ensures that we maintain balance in the Convent. Neither dwindling nor growing too fast. Progress is slow and steady. And those who are not mothers have other callings and gifts. Music, art, agriculture—you name it."

"What if they want to marry one of the men?"

"Marry?" Nora laughs. "We've moved beyond that old lie."

"Then how do the women and men . . ." Jude feels color rising to his cheeks and turns to the fire. "You know, procreate?"

"This is why we have sires, of course. They serve the Convent in their own way, by donating their seed. The best of their seed joins with the best of the mothers' eggs, and one of the mothers is chosen to carry the child to new life."

"Wait, there's no . . . mating?"

"Of course not! What a crude way to create life. We're not animals. Why would the Convent ever resort to that?"

Jude swallows, searching for the right word. "For pleasure?"

"What do you think we are?" Nora sounds surprised, but her cheeks blush.

"I have no idea what you are."

"When a mother pairs with a sire, if their genes are compatible, they can create new life. But who would act like an animal? It is better to maximize life through selection."

"How do you do this?"

"After the seed is given and paired, we can screen the embryos to choose those which are best."

"Even their gender?"

"Gender is a lie. We simply choose the best—those who contribute the most beauty and order to the Convent."

"So what do you do to the boys?"

"There are no boys at the Convent."

"Of course there are. Remember, you captured some of them. And I competed against them in that ceremony."

"Those we captured became citizens. We removed their venom."

"What's that supposed to mean?"

"We don't blame your kind for being born the way you are, but around twelve years old, the evil venom starts to surge in you. We save you from that."

Jude remembers when he first saw Nora, in the field,

crouching under a calf with a tool in her hand. "You castrate them."

"No, of course not. That was the violent way men used to do it. We have gentler methods to stop the evil. What matters is that, after the procedure, your kind are no longer a threat. They will join the Convent, where all are equal."

"Except for the mothers?"

"The mothers are equal to everyone else, but they have the duty of leading. Sires have the duty of providing seed. Citizens have the duty of tending our animals and fields."

"Okay." Jude takes a deep breath. "Let me try again. What do you do to the humans who are born with . . . parts like mine?"

Nora smiles. "I told you. We raise them to be citizens or sires."

"How do you choose which are which?"

"We monitor and test them carefully. You saw the final test. The citizens who remain eligible to become sires perform for the Convent in the ceremony. New sires are chosen in that way, from that select group."

"What happens to the citizens who are not chosen to be sires?"

"We put them at rest. Like we did with your brother."

"How?"

"It is a simple, painless procedure. We make the T cease."

"The T?"

"You know," Nora lowers her voice, as if someone were listening. "Testosterone."

"But it's only a hormone. It's natural."

"T is the source of all the world's evil. Just look at what's happened to me since I met you." She motions to her chafed wrists, torn dress, and swollen ankle.

"It wasn't all my fault. It's been an adventure."

"It's been a struggle. Men fight. They start wars. They kill."

"Not all of them. Many made the world better." Jude remembers Ma's words. "One good man can save the world."

"There are no good men."

"Haven't you read anything from history?"

"Your old books are full of men's lies."

"How about our favorite composer, Tchaikovsky?"

"A woman could have written his works. Women could have done everything men did. Men wouldn't let them. They used their violence and power to dominate for far too long. We'd have a thousand female Tchaikovsky's for the one that happened to break through men's terrible reign. How else do you explain the world wars, the genocides? Were women ever the cause of them?"

Jude searches for an answer. "Helen of Troy?"

"She wasn't the cause! She was only the subject. That's what women have been through history: *the subject* of men. But no longer at the Convent. Our society was created to transcend this evil history. And we have succeeded. We live in peace."

"You live in an artificial bubble. It's not real."

"How can you say that? You've been there. You

performed with me before the Convent. You saw our beauty. Our harmony."

"It's not natural."

"It could have been . . ." Nora sounds hurt. "You had a chance to pair with me. You ruined that."

Jude studies the fine lines of her cheeks, her nose. He could have stayed. They could have . . . paired. No, her people took Pa and Ma and Esau. They are the evil ones.

But Nora. She's not evil.

"Look," he says. "I'm sorry it worked out this way. If your people hadn't taken my family, none of this would have happened. But they did, and I'll trade you to get them back. You'll be back in your perfect Convent."

"Fine. I thought you might be better than this, but I was wrong." She hugs her knees and looks away. "You're still a boy. I hope you're the last one."

26

♀

Passage

THREE DAYS PASS. THEN A week, a month. The air grows colder. Leaves turn from yellow to brown and litter the ground. A hard north wind blows in a flurry of snow. Jude gathers sticks until they're almost gone from the island. He catches fish, but not enough. The jarred food dwindles. Time heals Nora's ankle, from the size of a cantaloupe to a plum to nearly normal.

She starts going out with Jude, helping him gather whatever wood they can find. They talk about the Convent and his family. She admires his devotion to them. She learns that he was born and raised in his remote cabin, isolated from the world. She almost feels sorry for what he lost.

But he still has the music.

His talent never ceases to amaze her. They play the violin in the evenings. He teaches her new chords, new techniques. Even she, raised in a place of beauty and song, never imagined such sounds. She asks how he learned, and his answers always go back to Ma and history's masters. He tells her that's all he needed, but she senses something else. There's something about him and his story that gnaws at her, some puzzle piece that's missing.

They finish the jar of peaches. The next morning they wake to frost on the ground and ice at the edges of the river.

Jude tells her it's time to go, if she's ready. She says she is.

They load up the canoe with the supplies they have left and the violin. They cast off when the sun is high. The wind whips hard and cold across the wide river.

Nora's tattered dress is worthless against the wind. She huddles in a blanket and studies Jude as he paddles. His shaved hair has grown out to short, dark locks. His same fingers that dance upon the strings manage the paddle well. Water swirls with each stroke. One side and then the other. The canoe moves slowly upstream, against the gentle current. He keeps his eyes ahead. He's been unusually quiet today.

They both know what's coming. But only Nora knows how it's sure to play out. The mothers will have a lookout there. They will come and take Nora and Jude back to the Convent, where he can reunite with his family. This whole adventure will be over.

It's for the good.

The sun dips to the bare trees. Jude keeps paddling.

"Will we camp for the night?" she asks.

"No. We'll be there soon enough."

He sounds tired. Nora has an idea. "Want me to take a turn until dark?"

He turns back with weary eyes, full of questions.

"We have the same goal now, right?" she asks.

"Okay." He hands her the paddle.

She takes a stroke under his gaze. After watching him do this, it should be easy. But it's harder than it looks. The water drags, and the current pulls against her. By the time the sun has dropped and the light fades, her arms and hands feel the effort. Still she paddles, refusing to admit that she's tired.

Jude leans back with his hands clasped behind his head. "You know, I never expected a girl to be like you."

Between heavy breaths, she replies, "What's that supposed to mean?"

"I knew from the start that you're beautiful. But I've learned you're smart and skilled and strong, too. Stronger than I am in some ways."

"Not with this." She blushes and eyes the paddle instead of him. "But thanks."

Darkness falls but she is warm inside. She tells herself it's from the paddling, not the boy's words.

When she yawns and yawns again, he offers to take another turn and she lets him. He paddles steady as ever through the night. Clouds block the moon and stars. She curls into the blanket and dozes off.

She wakes to the canoe bumping against the shore.

They've reached a gap in the trees at the riverbank. The frigid air blows a few flakes, white against the ink sky.

Jude jumps out. He holds out his hand to her. "This is it."

She's too sleepy to question why he whispers so low. She

takes his hand and climbs out. Her legs feel stiff.

"Here." He moves halfway up the bank and sweeps aside vines. There's a small wooden door. He pulls it open.

"What's inside?" Nora asks.

"A tunnel," he says. "It's the way to the cabin. Go on in and I'll follow."

She hesitates, eyeing the small the entrance. It seems strange to enter this way. He never mentioned it, but it never came up.

"It opens up in just a little ways. I'll be right behind you." He holds out the faint lantern that they brought from the cave. "You can take this."

She takes it and ducks inside, out of the snow. The walls are gray stone and rounded, like a tube. She has to move forward on all fours. Cold darkness presses around her. It smells like a tomb.

Jude pulls the door closed behind her. There's a metallic click. Then he follows close.

She takes a deep breath to calm herself, then presses on like a diver going down for pearls. Her shoulders and back brush against the stones as she goes and goes, with Jude shuffling behind her.

At last the tube opens. Nora stands and looks around in amazement. The lantern's light reveals a small room, like a perfect windowless cube. There's a plain cot and shelves along the walls with food and water and batteries and supplies and more books than she's ever seen in one place. The jars have the same handwritten script as those in their cave on the island.

On a table by the cot there's a framed picture. Nora picks it up and studies it. A mother, a father, and two boys—Esau and Jude. But it's the parents who make Nora's jaw drop.

Jude comes to her side. "See, not so bad, right?"

She holds up the picture to him. "Why didn't you tell me?"

"Tell you what?"

"About your parents."

"I did. What about them?"

"Didn't they tell you?"

"I don't know what you're talking about."

"Your Ma and Pa. They're from the Convent."

"What?" Jude steps back. "No."

"Yes, well definitely your Ma." Nora looks at the picture again and thinks of Lilith and Krystal and Selene. "She was a mother!"

27

♂

History

JUDE STUDIES THE PICTURE and swallows. Ma looks younger, fiercer, and even more radiant. "A mother?"

"Yes!" Nora says. "One of the twelve. I've seen a picture of her before. She's famous. She's one of the very few who left. It was before we were born, but everyone knows about her."

"So she ran away?"

"No, the Convent allowed it."

"I don't believe you."

"Think about it. Why else would they let you live here, within their territory? Why else would they come and visit?"

"They must have tolerated us. That's all."

"They *tolerated* you because they let your Ma leave! In rare situations, the Convent allows this if a mother and a sire insist. Your parents, they must have really loved each other. They asked to leave, to live a life on their own, and the Convent agreed."

"Then why did they burn down our home?"

The girl winces and looks down, as if guilty of something. "There's a condition if a couple leaves."

"What is it?"

"Their children belong to the Convent."

Nora's words click, like a final puzzle piece. Jude gazes at his parents in the picture and suddenly remembers Ma and Pa talking years ago. They were in front of the fire. They'd thought Jude was asleep. He came down for a glass of milk and listened to them.

The mothers won't harm us, Ma said. *The Capital would.*

You really think it's so bad there? Pa replied.

Yes, they started these sick experiments. We're protected here on Convent land. We have everything we need.

But the boys don't. They're getting older, Genevieve.

I know, Ma said.

The mothers could come any day . . .

I know. Ma's voice was thick, rising to a plea. *But we've kept them secret this long.*

Better for them to have freedom than not be boys at all. I'll take them to the Capital.

Just a little longer, John. Please.

Jude had been only seven or eight. Now it made sense. They'd kept Esau and him hidden, even as they hid the full truth from their sons. But why *hadn't* Pa taken them to the Capital? What did Ma mean about experiments?

Whatever their reasons, it ended in disaster. Hiding only lets truth rot and spoil. Now, unearthed by Nora, the truth about his parents is noxious. His blissful childhood was a lie.

Enabled by the Convent. He staggers to the cot and sits.

"You okay?" Nora asks.

His breaths are ragged. "No."

"What is it?" she asks, sitting down beside him. She is like a rose in a tomb.

"Maybe I'm not so different from you."

"Is that so bad? Like I've said, the Convent is the best humanity has come up with."

"No. Not for boys."

"But it is. You know about the world outside. You've read the books and heard the stories. Full of wars and tragedy and death, right? That's what testosterone did. The Convent saves us from that."

"Only by twisting nature. We were made to be different."

"That doesn't mean it's best."

Jude sighs. They've debated this a dozen times. "God created them male and female. The devil tempted Eve, and *she* ate the forbidden fruit. That's what cursed us all."

"The devil is testosterone."

"That's ridiculous."

"What do you think the devil is?" Nora asks.

"An angel who rebelled and was thrown out of heaven."

"Just as we throw testosterone out of the Convent."

"The Convent is built on lies."

"There are many shades of truth. All I'm trying to say is, you don't have to feel bad that your parents were from the Convent, too. We're more alike than I thought."

Jude forces a smile, even as he recoils at her words. She's

right, in a way. But his stories *are* real. He's seen it in nature over and over. Every species roams free, male and female, mating and propagating. Why should humans be different? Why does this girl make him feel the way he does?

He meets her eyes, resolved. He has to let her go. He has to give her up, if he's ever going to get his family back and learn the truth. But he needs to keep her hidden to have any chance when the mothers come.

"I hid here," he says. "You will too."

"You mean *we* will hide here?"

He shakes his head. "If I take you up there, they'll do whatever they want to me. Please stay here. I promise I'll come back."

"You expect me to trust you?"

"Yes, please. For my family."

Nora hesitates but slowly nods. "Come back soon. Okay?"

"Thank you. I will."

He starts to turn away. Then, fearing he might not see her alone like this again, that he might lose her, he risks something bold.

He leans toward her.

Quick as lightening. His lips on hers. Soft as a whisper.

Her hand goes to her mouth in surprise. He grins and leaves without a chance for her, or himself, to change their minds.

28

♀

Books

NORA FEELS DIZZY IN THE underground room, her steps echoing on the bare concrete.

What was that?

She agreed to Jude's plan. He had showed kindness. They had shared music and food. He seemed almost like a friend, and now she knows his parents came from the Convent. His mom had even been a mother. Maybe he isn't so bad, deep down, even if he is a boy.

But he kissed me!

She shakes her head in disbelief. This kind of thing would never happen at the Convent. It was never permitted.

Her fingers touch her lips, remembering. Her heart still races.

No, it was not exciting, she insists.

She tries to calm herself. She could have to wait a while before the mothers come to Jude. It's only a matter of time.

She eyes the small shelf of books beside the cot. There are

more than a dozen. She decides to pull out the thickest one first. It has sturdy leather binding and the spine says, *Holy Bible*.

She's heard of this book. She knows of its violence. It tells of man's cruel history of wars and killing, like so many other old books. They have no need for such terrible stories in the Convent. Praise the mothers for their daily videos, condensing this history in powerful form, saving them from dwelling on the evils of the past.

She starts at the beginning and reads a couple pages. It sounds like a distorted myth. Nothing like the true history recorded in the *Holy Word of the Convent*.

It says God created man first. Ridiculous. How could there ever be a man without a woman to give him birth?

It says God took a rib from Adam and made it into Eve. Nonsense. A woman is far more than a part of a man.

It says the man and woman became one flesh. Disgusting. God made humans to be greater than the animals, not to reproduce like them.

But then it says the first two children were boys, Cain and Abel, and Cain killed his brother. That part sounds right. And that is exactly why the Convent brings out the best in humanity—saving men from themselves, so all may have beauty and *peace*.

She goes back to the table of contents. There's one chapter called Ruth. She figures that, if it's about a woman, maybe it's closer to the truth.

It's not long, but it still takes a while to read. The room is silent beyond her own breathing and turning of pages. She stops midway through and snacks on a jar of pickled okra. There's enough jarred food to survive for a month.

The chapter about Ruth is interesting enough. But it only shows how broken things get when men roam free. For too long women let themselves become dependent on the crueler sex, and that caused far too many problems.

She puts the Bible back on the shelf and scans other titles. *The Odyssey, The Peloponnesian War, Paradise Lost.*

War, war, war. She's heard about these books and so many others like them. All diagnose the world from the perspective of men, and so they all get it wrong.

Instead she pulls out a book she's never heard of: *Jane Eyre*. It's the only one she sees by a woman, Charlotte Brontë.

She curls up on the cot and starts to read.

29

♂

Sire

JUDE CRAWLS OUT OF THE hidden tunnel and emerges into the remains of his home. The cold wind has swept away the clouds. The moon and stars cast silver light on the devastation. A chimney stands blackened and lonely. Around it are charred remains—ashes and burned metal things.

He kneels beside a jumble of pots and pans. He lifts the blade of a butcher's knife with a burnt-off handle. He shuffles to where the piano used to be. All that remains are metal parts and wires, warped by the blaze. The books, the pictures, the life. It's all gone.

He sits on the stone ledge of the hearth.

He thinks of Nora below. His lips tingle even as his heart tinges with guilt. Maybe he shouldn't have left her down there. No, it was the only way. *She'll be fine*, he assures himself.

But the sooner the mothers come, the better. He gathers wood and builds a fire. They'll see the smoke. They'll come.

The flames warm his back as the night deepens with no sign of the mothers. His stomach grumbles and he thinks of Ma. She always kept her kitchen clean and warm. How many meals did she serve him here? Hundreds, thousands. And now it's ashes.

He wipes at his eyes. He takes a deep breath. The mothers destroyed everything he knew, but he can't let emotion cloud his thoughts. He needs all his wits when they come. As Ma would say, *weeping may tarry for the night, but joy comes with the morning*.

He curls up before the hearth and sleeps. He dreams of Nora.

Morning dawns cold and windy and clear. It's the type of cold that whips through clothes and bites at bones. He piles more wood onto the coals and breathes the fire back to life. He eats and waits, but no one comes.

The sun rises. No one comes.

It's near dusk when he hears a buzz overhead. The hairs on the back of his neck stand up. A drone hovers a hundred feet above.

Figures appear at the edge of the trees. He counts five, then ten, then twelve. Three of them approach across the grassy field. They pass between a pair of young oak trees planted for Jude and Esau. Their three shadows stretch long, all the way to the forest, where the others stay hidden.

As the three draw closer, Jude realizes the middle person looks different. The two beside him wear white robes. But he wears a purple robe and is larger, with a dark shadow at the chin—a thick beard. The way the man walks is so familiar that Jude's stomach sinks. It's a man he saw in a photo last night but hasn't seen in person in years.

It's Pa.

"Son, ya look like ya seen a ghost," Pa says.

Jude feels part of himself retreat inside. He expected the mothers. He hoped they'd bring Esau or Ma, if they're still alive. But he never dreamed of Pa coming. Ma said Pa was gone.

This must be a trap.

But here Pa is, tall and bearded and smiling. He seems to command the respect of the two steely women standing beside him, like a Solomon of old, surrounded by wives. Jude can even smell him—tobacco, wood, spice, man.

"Surprised to see me?" Pa asks. "Well, it's been a while."

"I thought you were dead," Jude says.

"Nah, got caught up by these here women, but life's been good. They let me come out here to try to talk sense into ya. Where's the girl ya took?"

His voice is too slow, almost slurred. Pa never talked like this. Something's very wrong. "Ma said you were gone."

"Well, your Ma always was a wise one. They would've taken you and Esau. Instead they got me."

"They took Esau and Ma."

He runs a hand through his hair and sighs. "Well, it figures I guess, since we're on their land."

"This is *our* land," Jude says. "We plowed this land. We lived here." He looks away from Pa, at the trees around them.

"You planted those two trees for Esau and me."

"Those were good times, son. But the times are changin' round these parts. And trust me, life's not bad at the Convent."

"Not bad! They're the ones who burned our home. They took everyone from me. It's a prison!"

"Ya don't know that. It's been home to me. And they'll give ya another chance, son."

"What, to be a slave like you?"

Pa smiles patiently. He holds his arms forward. "I wear no shackles. I'm no slave."

This is all a lie.

This isn't the Pa he knew. They've changed him, drugged him, something. It's his body, but it's not really him. Jude looks to the older woman to Pa's right. She has stood still and silent, cloaked in a long white robe.

"What have you done to him?" Jude asks.

"Your father is a sire," the woman says.

Jude takes a step back, stunned. *The duty of providing seed*, Nora said. He stares at Pa and feels betrayed.

"Listen, son. All they want is the new mother."

"Nora," the woman says. "Where is she?"

Jude meets the woman's icy stare. She has short gray hair and a huge ruby at her neck. Her eyes look hard enough to break diamonds. "Where's Esau?" he asks. "Is Ma alive?"

"Of course she is," the woman says. "Is Nora?"

A flutter of hope. Ma really *is* alive. "Nora's fine."

"Show us Nora and we'll show you your family," the

woman says. "They're being brought here now."

"Prove it."

"You are testing my patience," the woman says, voice like a growl. "You kidnapped her. You contaminated her. You *ruined* her."

"No, I took care of her."

"Impossible. Not even our best could remain pure after so much time with your kind. You dragged her through these cold woods for weeks. We've tried to be patient. We brought your father to show you we can be fair. Now you must bring us Nora."

Jude looks from the woman to Pa. He feels trapped. If he gives them Nora, he'll lose everything.

"She's not here," Jude says.

"Then where is she?"

Jude shakes his head. "I'll tell you when you bring my family. Then we can make a trade."

"This is not a *trade*," the woman says. "This is an order."

"Come on, son," Pa says. "No more foolin' around."

"Last chance," the woman says.

"Or what?" Jude asks.

"Or you will lose everyone you love."

Jude swallows his fear. "Why are you doing this?"

The woman glares at him, then looks to the other woman. "I've had enough, Selene."

"Yes, Lilith." The other woman's round face is stern, like a boulder pressing down against Jude. "We will make this simple. Bring us Nora now or you will lose all that you have, one at a time. And you will end up in the same place: giving us Nora. This is your final chance to save your family and yourself."

The woman's challenge stiffens Jude's spine. Resolve surges up and truth tells him there is no easy way in life. He glances at Pa, content and hollow and broken. Pa is not who he once was. Maybe they forced him to do this. He didn't have what Jude has: leverage. He can't give that up. He can't let them have Nora. But he also needs time to figure out how to use that leverage.

"Leave now," he says. "And I will bring her to you."

The women exchange a glance. They look surprised. The one named Selene whispers to Lilith, "*She's not here . . .*"

"Tell us where she is, *now*," Lilith commands.

"I'll bring her. Just give me time."

"Very well," Lilith replies. "You wish to defy us. Your choice has consequences." She puts her hand softly on Pa's arm. "This won't hurt one bit."

Pa only smiles in response.

"Wait . . ." Jude says. "What are you doing?"

"Making sure you understand the seriousness of your choices," Lilith says. Then, without hesitation, she gracefully pulls out a syringe and plunges the needle into Pa's arm.

"Barely felt it," he says, as if it's routine.

But his face suddenly goes pale. A brief look of concern, a withdrawal of thought, flashes in his eyes.

Then he collapses, motionless.

"There now, *boy*." The cold woman holds the needle up

before Jude. A drop of blood falls from its sharp tip. "If you do not bring us Nora, your brother will share the same fate next. You have one week."

She and Selene turn with a sweep of their white robes and stride toward the ring of women at the forest edge. The sun has fallen below the horizon. The women, the devils, cast no shadows.

Jude rushes to his father and kneels.

"Pa," he says. "Pa!"

His father doesn't budge.

Jude knows but refuses to accept it. He presses his hand to Pa's wrist and neck and feels no pulse. He leans his ear over Pa's heart. All is still.

30

♀

Eulogy

NORA READIES TO SCOLD THE boy as she hears him shuffling through the passage to her underground cell. He left her for hours and hours, maybe days. She slept and read and slept some more. She finished *Jane Eyre*. Part of the story confirmed her views of men, full of danger and deceit, but other parts have shaken her. *Will I not guard, and cherish, and solace her?* Mr. Rochester said. The mothers never speak of men doing that. But it is only fiction. Jude is not Mr. Rochester from that fanciful old book.

He opens the door.

Nora rises to confront him. "Where have you . . ."

His reaction freezes her accusations on her lips. Shoulders slumped, eyes downcast. The light of the lantern makes his face haunting.

"What happened?" Nora asks.

"They killed him," Jude says.

"Killed who?"

"Pa."

"Your father?" Nora remembers the boy saying her father was already gone. "How is that possible?"

"They injected something. He's dead."

"*Who* did this?"

"Your people. Last night two women came in their white robes, with Pa in a purple robe. He looked like a king. They killed him and left."

White robes. The mothers. Purple robe. "Your Pa was a sire."

"Yes."

Nora knows there are times when a sire, like any old bull, has to be put down for the good of the herd. It's usually private and peaceful, but they wanted Jude to see this. They let him see his father before he passed.

"Did you talk with him?" she asks.

"Yes."

"It was a kindness. They've given him final rest."

"Kindness?" Jude looks up with a sudden fury in his eyes. He shouts at her, "They killed him!"

"It's a mercy to sires," she says calmly. "We save them from old age, from suffering. And we do it without pain."

The boy shakes his head, tears in his angry eyes. "I hate your people."

"You still don't know us. What else did they say to you?"

The boy doesn't answer. He lies on the cot with his back to Nora and his hands over his ears.

She asks more questions, but he ignores her. She even tells

him, "I'm leaving," and he doesn't budge.

She moves through the passage and up and out of the cell. The sky is blindingly bright after the long darkness, with the sun near its zenith. She rubs her eyes and drinks deep of the fresh air. As her eyes adjust, she sees the body.

A sire in a purple robe. Jude's father.

The mothers wouldn't do it this way. Unless . . .

This is where the boy brought her, to try to make a trade. The pieces come together. The mothers must have tried to convince Jude to tell where he'd hidden her. He must have refused.

She scans the field and forest in the distance. There's no sign of anyone.

"*Help!*" she shouts. "*I'm here!*"

Sparrows chirp back. A crow caws.

She yells out at the top of her lungs. She yells over and over. But no one responds. No motion stirs in the surrounding forests. Wouldn't they leave someone to watch the boy? Couldn't they guess the boy held her nearby? What did he say to them?

She goes to the forest and walks along its edges, occasionally calling out into the woods. Studying the ground and trees reveals nothing to her. Whoever came seems long gone.

The sun lowers toward the bare treetops.

She returns to the burnt cabin. If she's going to leave the boy and head for the Convent, she'll need supplies. She'll gather them up and go at dawn.

Jude is there when she returns. He sits in quiet vigil beside his father. A small fire crackles in the hearth.

He looks up as she approaches. "You came back."

"No one's here."

"I told you. They left."

Nora still doesn't understand why they wouldn't leave someone to watch for her. "What did they say about me?"

"They said I contaminated you and ruined you. I said I didn't hurt you at all and that I'd bring you to them."

Contaminated. No. Mother God, no.

Nora's hands cover her face. Her world spins.

That's why they left her. It's always a danger with T. Spend too much time around it and the venom can spread. They'll consider her lost and contaminated until she can prove otherwise.

She has to get back. Soon.

"Don't look so sad," he says. "I'll take you back to them. But would you help me first?"

"With what?"

"Building a pyre."

Nora finds herself, to her own surprise, agreeing. Jude needs help. She wasn't going to leave until morning anyway. It's a truce.

They spend the hour of dusk preparing. They gather wood to fill the base of the canoe. Then, together, they drag the man's body across the field to the riverbank. His dead weight is like a felled tree. They coordinate to lift him into the slender boat. It nearly sinks, bobbing just above the river's surface.

Dusk gives way to dark. They make torches from the hearth. They walk side by side, slow and ceremonious, to the river and canoe and corpse. The boy sings a haunting tune. Nora has never heard the words before.

Swing low, sweet chariot,
Coming for to carry me home.

Their torches ignite the wood in the canoe. They shove it out of the shallows. Cold water nips at their feet as flames rise into the dark night. The current turns the pyre and pulls it gently downriver, drifting beautiful and fleeting as a lost dream.

It's almost out of sight when Jude speaks. "He was a good Pa." The words come as if fully formed in hours of silent work. "We all have fallen short of the glory of God. He fell far from grace, but grace knows no limit. Faithfully he loved until he left. Not until the end, but may the coals stored up in brighter years still burn through the darkness. Goodbye, Pa. I love you. Goodbye."

Nora feels tears in her eyes. "That's beautiful."

"Fire dazzles as it destroys."

She puts a hand gently on his shoulder. "Are you okay?"

"There's nothing left for me here."

"So we'll be heading back together?"

He looks at her for the first time in hours. Tears streak his cheeks, but a faint smile grazes his lips in the torchlight. "I guess you'd never make it without me."

"Oh?"

"This time we'll be walking."

"You don't have to come."

"But I will," Jude says. "I could still save Ma and Esau."

31

♂

Venom

THE DAY AFTER THE FLOATING pyre took Pa away, Jude and Nora set out toward the Convent. The sky is solemn gray, as if a vast blanket lays over the earth. It's unusually warm, too. Insects buzz about, squirrels chatter—the recent frost and flurries forgotten. But Jude has learned better than to trust an Indian summer, as Ma calls it. He packs extra supplies and coats. Nora wears a pair of Ma's sturdy pants and a shirt that they found in the cellar.

They wade through the sticky air through the morning. Their packs and emotions make it slow going. They make it only a few miles before the afternoon. The sun is still hidden behind clouds when they stop at a hilltop glade.

"Nice view," Nora says, dropping her pack to the ground. "Can we rest here?"

"Fine." Jude recognizes the place. It's where Esau paused when he and Jude left home together. Esau had seen a wild buck. Jude yearned to see a real live girl. Now she's here, beside him.

But the green forest has lost its leaves. Jude has lost his family.

They eat a little in silence. The violin stays in its case. The bare forest whispers around them. A turkey rustles past.

He puts the food away and stands. "We should keep going."

"Fine." Nora lifts her bag and groans. "You really think we'll need all this? It's not that far."

"Winter is coming," Jude says. "We could get there in a couple days, or it could snow."

"Doesn't feel like snow." Nora sighs. "At least our bags get lighter at each stop."

"Be glad we don't have to haul our water, too." Jude gazes down the ridge to the river, leading to the lake in the distance. The Convent is not far from there. "We'll try to reach the lake by night."

They don't make it that far. Dusk comes sooner than it did when Esau and Jude came this way. They set up camp by a pile of boulders. The temperature drops. Nora huddles close to the fire and hugs her knees.

"You alright?" Jude asks.

"I'll be fine. I'm just cold and tired."

He watches her for a few minutes, shivering and pale. He closes his eyes and thinks. If only her people had done what he asked, she'd be back with them and he'd be with Ma and Esau. They'd be rebuilding their cabin and life would move on.

Love your enemies, Ma would say.

But they're terrible, Jude replies in his mind. *I have to fight them. I have to get revenge.*

Love your enemies . . .

Jude opens his eyes and tries to sees the girl differently. She's probably hurt and afraid. The mothers abandoned her. He takes a deep breath and rises. He moves around the fire and sits close beside her, with his blanket wrapped around them both.

After a while in quiet, the girl says, "You're still angry at me."

"Yeah."

"The mothers did it," she says. "Not me. I swear, I would never do what they did."

Jude turns to her in surprise. "Really? You said you'd become a mother. You said this is what happens to sires."

"I know, but I'd never seen it. I didn't imagine it would be so . . . so harsh."

"You said the chemical was painless."

"For the one who dies, but . . ." Her amber eyes glisten as she studies Jude. "I see how much it hurts you."

Jude turns and stares at the fire. He wipes his eyes. He won't give her the satisfaction of being right. Loving your enemy doesn't change that they're the enemy. It just means you share a blanket and wait until the right time to fight.

He can wait. And for now he can share warmth. He lies down with his back to the girl, and she follows his lead without a word. The only sounds are their breathing and the soft crackle of the fire warming them together beneath the blankets.

The next morning mist wraps around them. Neither speaks much as they pack up and continue the trek.

Within an hour the mist lifts like a veil. Dew dries and leaves crunch under their feet with the steady march. Flocks of black birds soar overhead, migrating south. The sun burns through the clouds. The brisk hike, loaded with supplies, tires them both. But they press on in silent competition.

They reach the lake by midday. The water is alluring. Jude strips down to his undershirt and washes off his face and arms.

Nora does the same, with her back to Jude. She wears a black tank top. She raises her arms high toward the sun—arms so long they could be ropes pulling the sun closer. Or maybe the sun just wants to be closer. Jude sure does.

She turns and catches him staring at her. "Do I still look dangerous to you?"

"No. I mean, why would you ask that?"

"You look nervous."

He pretends like he's not embarrassed and starts pulling out food from his pack. "We should eat," he says. "We still have a long way to go."

"You know, you've changed since you kidnapped me."

"Me? You're the one who changed."

"You didn't know me then. You think you do now?"

"I know more." Jude hands Nora an apple, then takes a bite of his own.

"But you can't truly know a person without understanding where they're from."

"I think I'll learn more than I'd like when we get there."

A playful smile lifts her lips. "We could sneak in without being noticed."

"Sneak in? Why would you do that?"

"I've been thinking about what you said, about how they called me contaminated. It's not good. It means they might have selected another mother to take my place. I'd like to learn more before we reveal that we're there."

"It doesn't make sense. I told them I didn't hurt you. As far as I can tell, you're not contaminated."

"Thanks," she says. "But you're still dangerous."

"Yeah, I know, full of T. Is that why you stayed with me?"

"Let's not go too far."

They exchange a quiet, understanding smile. They eat together. The sun shines through the trees and shimmers on the lake. They could be young lovers out for a picnic, catching a glimpse of paradise on earth.

Nora steps away to relieve herself. She's out of Jude's sight when she lets out a yelp.

Jude rushes toward her. "What . . . ?"

"Ow, ow!" She's swinging wildly at her legs.

A blur of yellow and black swarms up around her.

His stomach sinks. Yellow jackets buzz around her in a rage. She must have stepped on a hive.

Run, his mind screams.

But what if she's allergic too? Her hurt grabs him like a

fist around his heart and yanks him forward.

Please God don't let me die . . .

He charges in and picks her up and runs for the lake. Through the adrenalin he doesn't feel the two stings that prick him, one to his left ankle and another to his right hand. His only thought is to get away and get underwater. The bees trail after them like a haze of exhaust.

Jude leaps into the lake with Nora, dipping fully under the cool surface. The bees return home, victorious.

"They're gone now," Jude says, meeting Nora's eyes as they both peek out of the water's surface. "You alright?"

She winces as she scans around. "It hurts," she says. "They stung me all over."

"I don't think they got me."

"Really? That's a miracle."

"Thank God." Jude lets out a heavy sigh. "I'm allergic."

"What? Then why on earth did you come after me?"

"I don't know. They were hurting you." He smiles at Nora and feels a strange mix of pride and humility in rescuing her. "Shall we go back and burn their hive to smithereens?"

Nora laughs uneasily. "Let's not. But let's make camp and stay near the water. I don't feel like walking anymore today."

"Good plan." Jude lies on his back and floats toward the lake's edge and starts to feel something wrong.

His hand stiffens. Then his leg and arm.

His throat dries, tightens, burns.

He stops in the shallows on all fours, gasping for breath.

Nora swims past him and comes out of the water. She

turns back. "Jude?"

He can't answer.

"Jude?" She hurries back to him. "What's wrong?"

He chokes out, "stung . . ."

Horror washes over her face. "What should I do?"

He lifts a rigid, trembling arm and points up the hill beside the lake. "Cave."

"You want to go there?"

He nods, head tilting.

"Okay, let's go."

He tries to rise, but wobbles and collapses. She rushes to him as he falls. He lands in her arms motionless.

"Jude. *Jude*?"

He doesn't answer.

Breath rasps through his lungs.

32

♀

Nurture

NORA'S HEART POUNDS AS SHE drags Jude's heavy, motionless body away from the lake's edge. She's almost to shore when a rock slips under her foot. She falls in the shallows. She's soaked. Her teeth chatter and her body shivers.

He's barely breathing.

She uses all the strength she has to pull him from the lake and the bees and toward the hill, like Jude said.

He's pale as snow.

She shifts position, grabbing Jude from behind, holding him under the arms, and dragging him backwards.

She pulls him up the hill, foot by exhausting foot. Sweat drips from her brow when they reach a rocky outcrop. She finds the opening to a little cave and lays him inside.

"Don't die," she pants. "I'll be right back."

She stumbles back down the hill. She retrieves the bag from the lake's edge and returns to the cave. The boy lies still, eyes closed, breath faint.

"I'll build a fire," she says.

Her hands tremble as she gathers a small pile of dry leaves and twigs. The match strikes true and burns like life. Soon the blaze lights up the cave. The warmth gives her hope.

He'll survive. He has to survive.

She manages to get some water into his lips. She knows about allergies, of course. The Convent teaches of their danger, from pollen to peanuts to bees. No one with serious allergies could become a mother. Too risky.

She looks over Jude and finds two swollen spots. His hand and ankle are red and puffy. She doesn't know how to stop the reaction. It's not like snake venom that can be drawn out. Maybe it just takes time.

She gathers enough wood to last a day and builds up the fire. By then she's too tired to do anything else. She lies next to the boy and falls asleep.

She wakes once in the night. Outside the cave the stars wink at her like old friends.

Please, Mother God, let him survive.

A star shoots across the sky, as if answering, telling her it will be okay. She adds a few more logs to the fire and sleeps again.

It's dawn when she wakes. She goes to Jude.

His breaths are shallow and faint, his skin wan. He looks like he hasn't budged since she laid him down. She refuses to admit that he looks like a corpse.

"Jude?" she whispers.

No answer.

She decides to make everything as comfortable as she can for him. She roams the hillside and gathers soft leaves. She bundles long golden grasses from the lake's shore. With these she builds a bed, soft and gentle. Each time she returns she puts a log on the fire, too. Its coals burn steady.

By night she's exhausted. She eats a bit of the food they've brought and realizes Jude has eaten nothing. She goes to the lake and fills a jar of water. She pours what she can into his mouth.

She lies down but tosses and turns, trying to release her fear that the fire, or the boy, might fade. When she wakes she checks him first. There's been no change at all. Log on the fire. Sleep.

She spends the next day doing more of the same, thinking, then avoiding thoughts by hauling wood or water. That night she sits by the fire and studies Jude's still face. He has fine features for a boy. He looks gentle, pristine, like a porcelain doll.

"I'll play you a song," she says.

It takes her a while to tune his violin. She practices a few notes and then falls into the music. Time fades. The walls of the cave glow and echo her solemn notes.

The boy doesn't stir.

She cries as she puts the violin down and falls asleep.

The third morning she decides she has to get help. He won't survive if he can't eat. She sets to preparing things. She stacks extra wood. She packs enough food for her for a few days and lays the rest close to the boy. She covers him with a blanket.

Now she stands over him, ready to leave.

"I'll get help," she whispers. "It's for your own good."

His still, sick body doesn't respond. She feels something hard, like a lump in the throat. He started all this, kidnapping her and dragging her into these wilds.

But he doesn't deserve to die. She'll get help.

"It's for your own good," she says again.

She turns and walks away. The clouds stretch like fabric in the blue sky—indigo dyed red then orange with the sunrise.

Red sky at morn, the boy would say.

Nora heads east, to the Convent, to help. A pair of ducks soars overhead, flying south.

A raft of ducks, Jude would say.

The sun has risen well above the trees and begins to descend when Nora reaches a steep ridge. She climbs up the slope, using her hands to steady herself. At the top she pauses to rest. She eats one of the eggs she brought—that Jude brought—and warms in the sun's midday brilliance.

The ridge gives her a sweeping view. To the west there's a hint of clouds rising, the distant, dark clouds of a storm. More important, to the east, she spots something white by the river winding through the forest.

The Convent. So close.

She could reach it before night, or least tomorrow.

A robin chirps so close to Nora it makes her jump.

Do not worry about tomorrow, Jude would say. *Today has*

enough trouble of its own.

She doesn't mean to, but she looks back. Below, near the glistening lake, a thread of smoke snakes up from the cave where she left him.

Today has enough trouble.

She sighs and her hand covers her mouth. She does not want to feel this. She belongs in the Convent. She is a mother.

Was a mother.

Contaminated. That's what the mothers said.

If that's what the Convent decided, she could be demoted. Everything she's worked for could be gone. She doesn't want to believe it, but it's the only thing that explains why they didn't wait for her at the burned cabin. Surely they could have found her by now. They must be able to see the smoke.

The robin sings again. Today Jude needs help.

As much as she doesn't want to admit it, part of her reason for leaving to get help was to get herself back to the Convent. She realizes the Convent would help him but also take his freedom, and more. He wouldn't want that. He wanted her, not the Convent. He charged into the bees for her, knowing what might happen. He risked his life for her.

The robin flies off and Nora goes the same direction, back toward Jude. The clouds roll in with the afternoon, the great dark clouds of a storm suddenly swelling and casting a shadow over the forest.

Thunder rumbles by the time she reaches the boy. She finds him in the same place, helpless and shivering, chest rattling with every breath.

She dabs his forehead.

"I brought help," she says. "Me."

The storm flashes violence across the sky and drops hail the size of marbles, pelting the cave wall and putting out the fire. Even after the lightning and thunder pass, freezing rain remains. Nora hardly notices. She falls into deep sleep beside the boy, the peaceful slumber of someone being where they're supposed to be.

The next morning, through a bitter cold mist, Nora sets to work. She improves the lean-to shelter against the cave entrance and rebuilds the fire, her sheer willpower and dozens of matches overcoming the waterlogged wood.

She treks down the muddy slope to the edge of the lake. She dips her bucket into the frigid water and returns slowly, patiently up the hill, trying not to spill a drop. She has all the time in the world but very little hope.

Soup can help with hope. She cooks in the little pot that the boy brought. She adds a dash of salt and beans from a can. It simmers and smells like heaven. She manages to get a few spoonfuls into the boy. She eats the rest.

The boy lives but does not improve. Neither does she.

A day passes. Then another.

The boy sleeps in fits. The only change is a clammy sweat forming on his skin. When he twists or mumbles in pain, she sings quiet songs. He does not respond except, at times, to whimper and fall silent again. That's better than the nothingness that came before. Until his bodily functions start to return, if erratic and limited. She cleans up, because no one else can. It's not so different than one of the mothers caring for a newborn. Or so she tells herself.

She marks the days on the cave wall. A new line scratched each morning. It is a challenge and a promise and a hope of sanity. This is a new day. Another day to survive.

33

♂

Dreams

THE SWAN IGNORES THE FIRST crow that swoops at it. They are opposites—one for grace and beauty and pure white, another for cawing and carrion and pure black.

"Away," the swan honks.

The crow soars off, cawing like laughter, like a call to arms.

And the call spreads. Caw, caw, caw.

Tens, hundreds.

Cawing and swooping like a rain of terror, of murder.

They strike at the swan, who fights for its life. Wings like seraphim spread and soar, only to be beaten downward by a dozen talons. A smooth surface of water is below.

With the violence of a falcon, the swan swipes its sharp beak at the attackers. They bay and bend back, but return in a mass of blackness.

They pelt down in fury. Too many, too much.

The swan's right wing breaks. Its neck bleeds, red on

white.

Sensing the end, the swan gives up the fight. It cannot win in the air. It must sink and rise again, when the killers have left.

Without any grace or calm, the swan ducks its head down and dives straight at the water. It plunges under the water's surface, where no crow will follow. In that stillness and quiet and dark, the swan rests, knowing that life will come again if only it can rise.

Murder, the swan thinks. *They call a group of them a murder.*

34

♀

Adversity

NORA STARES AT THE MARKS on the cave wall in despair. She counts them, then counts again. Nine scratches of gray on gray. Nine days of suffering and survival.

"We can make it another," she says, glancing at the pale boy. Her voice sounds far more determined than she feels, so much so that she laughs. Putting on a show for an audience that cannot see or hear.

She takes up a rock and scratches her tenth mark and goes outside. The sky is gray, the clouds heavy. As usual she goes to the lake first. It's the coldest morning yet. It looks like snow.

The still water shows few signs of life. The birds have gone quiet. Once, at dusk on the sixth day, Nora heard an approaching whir, louder and louder. She expected a drone, searching for her, but instead a helicopter soared over the lake from the south. It was so rare, but she felt sure it came from the Capital, maybe even visiting the Convent. It roared as it flew straight over her without slowing. She cried harder that night. She's looked every day since and seen no other signs of searching, of hope.

She fills the bucket and trudges back up the hill.

At the mouth of the cave she senses something different. It's a sound. Inside.

She peers through the mouth of the cave at the boy's spot. He's moved, sitting up and hugging his knees. She rushes in and kneels. The ground is still warm where he laid.

Her hands go to his arms, his cheek, his hair. He's alive and his eyes are open and she can't believe it.

"Jude," she says, through tears. "I was so worried . . ."

"Nora," croaks his voice, faint and raspy.

"Jude, Jude. Here, lie down now, not too much at once. You've eaten so little. We need to take it slowly, okay?"

"Okay."

She helps him lie back down on his bed. She takes a cloth and dampens it in the bucket and wipes his forehead. She turns and looks at the cave and sees the coals and the jars of food and the boy's eyes, watching her.

"Stay right there," she says.

"Okay."

She rushes about, building up the fire and thinking about what to feed him.

"Soup," she says. "Would you like soup?"

He nods.

She decides on a heartier recipe. She puts in some of the dried pork and opens a brand new jar of greens. She boils water in the pot and mixes it together and fills the cave with the smell of life and vigor.

"You've had a few spoonfuls here and there, but it's been so hard. So very little of it went down. It was like your body was gone, even though your breath remained. But you stuck with it. I'm proud of you, Jude. You fought and you didn't give up and you're here now. You're alive!"

"What . . . happened?"

He doesn't remember. This is a bad sign.

"Bees," she says. "You tried to save me and they stung you. Your ankle and hand got all swollen and, well, you're—"

"Allergic. Yes, bees . . ." He looks down at his hands as if seeing them for the first time.

"You were unconscious, barely breathing sometimes. But we've made it now. We have the cave and the fire, and you're awake, right?"

"Yes. Miracle." A weak smile spreads over his pale face. "Thank you."

"Well, yes. We'll get to that, I suppose. I tried to leave once. Not to abandon you. I wanted to get you help. I'm not a nurse or doctor. I've never seen anyone so out of it as you were. So I thought I'd just go to the Convent. It's not far away, you know. A day or two only. And I got almost there and you sent a robin to talk to me. And—"

"A robin?" he interrupts.

"Yes! A robin. I'm not that crazy, don't worry. Maybe a little. This cave will do that. Anyway, the robin was there singing when I first laid eyes on the Convent again. And I remembered what you said, about how God feeds the sparrows, and it was like you were there, calling me back. I know you don't like the Convent. And I guess I've thought about it a lot and I can kind of see why, after, you know, what happened to your Pa."

The cave falls quiet. Jude blinks his long lashes. "Crows."

"What?"

"Crows . . . try to murder the swan."

"I don't understand," Nora says.

"A dream, I think. Like what the mothers did to Pa. We fear what's different."

"That's true. I was afraid of you, at first. But then you were hurt, vulnerable. I saw we're not so different. Then I feared your weakness even more than your strength. I could hardly bear it."

"Thank you."

"You already said that."

"I'll say it again. Thank you. I'm alive."

She smiles and turns to the soup. "It's done, I think." She holds out a spoonful to him. "Here, try a sip."

He takes it down smoothly. "Good. More, please."

She fills a whole bowl and he manages to eat every drop.

"I'm tired," he says.

"Yes, of course. No need to rush it. You've got time to recover. It's all going to be okay now. I should let you sleep, but you have to promise me something, okay?"

"What?"

"You have to wake up again. Soon."

35

♂

Plans

JUDE CAN HARDLY STAND, LEANING against the cave wall, but it's worth it for the surprise. He woke as Nora went out this morning with an empty bucket. First, he managed to get to his knees. Then, slowly, to his feet. His vision spun as he tried to take a step, so he gave up on following her. But not on giving her a little surprise. He hears her coming back and grins, proud of being upright. A human again.

She appears in the cave entrance. The full bucket strains her arms, her knuckles white on the handle. When she glimpses Jude, she nearly drops it. Water sloshes out as she sets it down.

"Hey!" she says. "What are you doing up?"

"Good morning," he croaks.

She moves closer to him. "I'm glad you're awake. But you need rest. Lie down."

Jude yawns. "I've had enough sleep for a month."

"True." Her eyes meet his, brightly curious. She points to the rock wall behind him. "Count the marks."

Jude studies the scratches on the dimly lit cave wall. They are neatly organized in groups of five, like the work of a careful student doing tallies for homework, not like a girl stranded in a cave with an unconscious boy. The total number doesn't make sense. There are twenty scratches— four sets of five.

"No way I slept twenty hours," he says. "It was midday when . . . the bees. So it would have to be night. But it's been morning again. Was I out a whole day?"

Nora's face flashes concern. "Lay down. I will tell you."

"Okay," Jude says.

He steps away from the cave wall on legs of jelly. He stumbles and starts to fall. Nora catches him, her shoulder propped under his arm.

"Thanks," he breathes out, as she guides him a few feet over to the pallet where he woke up.

"You stay still and listen," she says.

He looks up at her helplessly. He can't resist her. He remembers the emotions that swirled over him before—they are vivid and clear, like a lighthouse through the fog. He yearned to be with her. But he didn't imagine he'd be unable to walk. All he can do is try to smile and nod.

"You know, you're cuter with your eyes open," she says.

"I missed seeing you."

She waves his comment away like it's a mosquito. "You were out for days. Then, after you first woke up, you've been in and out, just enough for a bite to eat before you slept a long time again. Each mark on the wall is a day."

Jude feels his chest tighten. "That's . . . almost a month."

"I told you."

Jude gazes up at her in amazement. The cave opening lets in light like a halo over her head. A memory emerges. She performed on stage. She chose him, and he took her away. The Convent . . . they took Esau and Ma . . . and they killed Pa. They're enemies. She's an enemy. The mothers told him to bring her back within a week . . .

"I'm too late. They'll kill Ma and Esau."

"No," she says. "I mean, we are too late, but they won't hurt them. They'll accept them into the community. I swear."

He meets her sincere eyes. He wants to believe her.

Love your enemy, he was taught. She's right here, and it's never been easier. "You could have left. Why'd you help me?"

"I couldn't let you die. It wouldn't have been right."

"But I . . . kidnapped you."

"Among other things . . ."

"I'm sorry," Jude says. "I'll make it up to you. I'll take you back. I'll trade you for Ma and Esau, like they wanted."

"I've been thinking about that," she says. "I have a plan. But first you have to get better."

"I know. I will. Then what?"

"You still want your Ma and brother, right?"

"Of course."

"So we'll go back to the Convent. When we get there, I'll go in alone, ahead of you. And then—"

"Hold up," Jude says. "No way that'll work."

"Hear me out. You said the mothers called me contaminated, right?"

"Yes."

"Mothers must be pure. Nothing else can satisfy Mother God. There's no forgiveness if the male species contaminates. It's not like your old books. It's . . ."

"What?"

"I don't know, but maybe . . ." Nora looks deeper into Jude's dark green eyes, in disbelief at what she's about to say. "Maybe you're right. Maybe there's something about the Convent that's wrong. I need to learn more. So that's why I thought of this plan. Now, listen, what if I *had* really left you here? I'll tell the mothers that you kept me tied up, but then you got hurt or sick or something. I escaped and came straight to the Convent. Once I'm there, I'll find out where your Ma and brother are, then I'll lead the mothers out to find you. While we're gone, you sneak in and rescue your family."

Jude feels too small, too weak to pull it off, but he doesn't have a better idea. A frontal assault certainly wouldn't work. Still, he sees more problems than hopes with this plan. "How many of the mothers do you expect to come for me? There were only a few who came to my family's cabin."

"Right. Only a few. But the ones who stay will have their guard down. The last thing they'll expect is for you to come while you're out in the forest hurt."

"How will I know where to find Ma and Esau?"

"We'll come up with a signal—some way to

communicate once I return with the mothers."

"Like what?"

"The Convent is not so big. There are only a dozen or so buildings. You can hide out and wait for me to say a key word in a certain place. Let's go with *Vivaldi*. After I say that, I'll say the name of a note to tell you which building your mother's in."

"I don't know the buildings."

"I'll teach you. And then I'll say some other code word to tell you where they are in the building."

"What if they're in different places?"

"They will be. We'll come up with a system."

"This could take a while."

She smiles down at him. "We've got time. You don't look like you're ready to go anywhere."

"Guess not."

"So get comfortable. We've got work to do."

36

♀

Warmth

NORA WAKES TO PERFECT QUIET. She sits up and glances to the pallet where Jude sleeps. He's not there. His blankets are ruffled and tossed aside. The fire's down to faint coals. The bucket is gone.

Outside a smooth layer of snow blankets the forest. The sky is cold and gray and dotted with large flakes. There are no birds chirping. No insects. No sign of life. Whatever tracks the boy left have already been covered by snow.

She eyes the spot where the bucket usually sits. *Did he go to get water in the snow? Foolish!*

He's been recovering well. She's spent the last two days telling him every detail he needs to know about the Convent. Where the sires are kept. When the Convent gathers each day, leaving places unguarded. What the layout of buildings looks like. How to navigate his way in and out. And on and on.

But none of that makes the boy ready yet. He left his bag and didn't even tend the fire. He's probably just trying to help, or to get some fresh air. He's been getting more restless in their little cave. He's bound to return soon.

She takes a deep breath and resolves to show enough wisdom for the both of them. First she has to add fuel to the fire. She stacks the wood high until it's crackling warmly. Then she sits and stirs through the boy's bag. There's his gun, his violin, and their remnants of food. Some jarred apples, bits of cheese, and only two pickled eggs left. She eats an egg.

With her hunger sated and the fire burning brightly, she should feel good. But she can't shake a troubling feeling about the boy. He's still too weak to make it far, much less in this weather.

She decides to head out after him. She takes the straightest path down to the lake, where she guesses he would have gone. The snow fills the sky like a wool blanket, blocking vision beyond a stone's throw. It's piling up and up, and each step takes more work, like she's trudging through a swamp. It's already up to her ankles.

When she reaches the lake's edge, the boy is nowhere in sight. But the bucket is there. She goes to it and sees the wooden container is half full, sitting on the snow.

Where is he?

The lake's surface is glass, swallowing up snowflakes. No way the boy went into the water. She studies the area around the bucket more carefully and notices a faint footprint. It leads to another step and another, each one almost fully covered in snow. He couldn't have left long ago.

Nora follows the tracks up a steep, rocky slope. The hill

rises to the right of where their cave is, in an area she hasn't explored. The tracks stay close to a tiny creek, only a few inches wide. It winds its way up a slender valley between two steep ridges.

The flurry thickens. It turns to blizzard.

Nora can barely see her hand in front of her face, much less the fading tracks. But she knows he's close, if only she can keep going uphill toward the rocks. She stumbles once and falls over a downed tree. She rises like a frosted mummy and presses on, with her face low to detect the slight impressions of footprints.

Where does he think he's going!

The tiny creek disappears under a giant boulder ahead of her. Large gray stones stand like monoliths among the pure white snow. The faint tracks weave in and out of the stones, almost aimless, like the boy wandered through with his eyes closed.

She trudges around the boulders once, twice. Each step makes her fears rise. She considers going back. The snow eases slightly, which allows her to see that her own tracks have been covered.

Did I miss something? Did he go somewhere else?

She slows down. She crouches and circles the boulders more carefully, like a hound sniffing its way forward. At one point, two boulders press together, forming a wall, but at the very bottom there's a hole. It can't be more than two feet wide. She drops to her belly, in the cold, muddy snow, and crawls through. The hole forms into a tiny tunnel, dark at the center but with light at the other end. She crawls out the other side and stops in disbelief.

Steam rises from a small pool of water. The boy is there, lying in the shallows with his back to her, as if in deep sleep.

She's tempted to pick up a stone and throw it at him. It takes some nerve to leave without a word in a snowstorm. But she's also relieved. At least he's alive. And the water looks warm.

She dips a finger in. It almost scalds, like a hot bath.

She takes off her coat and slips quietly and gradually into the water. Her only sound is a slight gasp as the hot spring greets her frigid skin. She sinks all the way under and smiles.

Okay. No wonder he didn't come back . . .

When her head comes up, the boy is staring at her. He has slipped under the water so that, like her, only his head and shoulders show.

"You found me," he says.

Face to face. Steam between them. His dark locks moist.

No, he's not cute. He's a fool.

"You left me. In a blizzard."

"I'm sorry. I was trying to help. I need to get stronger."

"You're still too weak. You went too far."

"I know, but listen. When I woke up, there were big snowflakes coming down. You were curled under your blanket. You looked so peaceful and warm. So . . . beautiful."

She splashes at him. "Get to the point."

He laughs and wipes the water from his eyes. "I didn't want to disturb you, and I knew it would get harder every minute to find dry fuel for the fire, and to get food and water. An inch of snow already covered the ground. So I saw the bucket and made up my mind to fill it up like you usually do."

"Foolish."

"Maybe, but when I left our cave, the cold air gave me a rush. Snow this thick is dangerous. I knew if it kept coming down, we'd be holed up for days. So I made my way down to the river. I leaned over to fill my bucket and knew I'd made a mistake. I . . ."

His voices chokes up.

Reluctant sympathy washes over Nora. "What happened?"

"I saw my reflection in the water. I barely recognized myself. So thin and pale. A few whiskers, too. The face looking back reminded me of Pa."

"I'm sorry."

He wipes his eyes. "Well, anyway, I scooped up some water and made the face go away and splashed myself. I looked around, watching the snow fall, and realized I'd been in that exact spot before. I glanced up the hill and saw this cluster of rocks at the top. Then I knew I had to get here, to the hot spring."

"You've been here before?"

"A long time ago. Esau and I were out exploring and playing hide and seek. I clambered into the rocks to hide, in a nook so small Esau might not fit. That's when I found it. A steaming pool. It was too hot then, in the middle of summer. Now it could be a lifesaver."

"You're still too weak for what you did. You could have frozen to death."

"I guess I got lucky. I made it here, didn't I?" He holds out his arms and swirls the water. "It's like paradise. Amazing, right?"

"It is," Nora admits. "You planning to stay here a while?"

"It's still snowing."

"We shouldn't let the fire go out."

"You're right. Let's go together. But let's warm up more first."

37

♂

Eden

SNOW FALLS AGAIN THE NEXT DAY. And the next. Inches pile on the frozen surface, up to their thighs. Jude and Nora walk back and forth to the spring, carving a direct path through the drifts and over the ridge. It doesn't take long once they've worn the path. The hikes give Jude exercise, letting his legs strengthen, his mind clear.

He starts to think of the hot spring as their personal Eden. He imagines the first man and woman, living in a garden. Maybe they had a hot spring like this one.

He and Nora develop a little ritual. She tells him to look away while she slips down to her undergarments and enters the water. Once she's fully submerged, she looks away while he does the same and eases into the steaming spring. They do the opposite when they leave.

He really does try to look away every time. But how can he expect to be perfect around Eve? He figures it's like that fruit Adam ate. A man can only resist so long.

Leadeth me not into temptation, he mutters under his breath.

Nora seems to know it. She almost flaunts it.

"Won't you grab my blanket?" she says, steam curling up from her shoulders and around her pixie hair that has grown longer around her ears.

He climbs out of the spring and puts on his outer clothes and gets her blanket.

"Hold it for me, but no looking!" she says.

He stares at the sky as she climbs out and wraps the blanket close. "Thank you," she says, smiling at him, melting him.

The schedule stays the same day after day. Wake up, feed the fire in the cave, and check the trap. Jude had only one trap in his pack, but it's enough to catch a critter every other day or so—mostly squirrels.

Jude does the messy work of killing and skinning and cooking. Nora starts to collect the skins and sew them together. She makes fur pillows for both of them, softening their cave.

Once the fire and food have been addressed, they hike together to the spring and slip into the water. They talk through all this, chatting about the forest and music and everything under the sun. The conversation comes easy, interspersed with comfortable moments of quiet.

Neither of them talks much while they're in the spring. It's part modesty, part fatigue. The pool is just large enough for them to float in their own half of the water, always out of reach. When their skin prunes and the sun descends, they return at dusk and have a bite of food. Jude is exhausted by then. He leaves his fiddle untouched. He sleeps long, dreamless nights, nearly hibernating.

Days pass in this strange routine. After a week, the snow has melted into little pools of white in the brown forest. Then another blizzard comes and drops another foot. They venture further and further to collect enough wood to keep their fire alive.

They've added another forty notches to the cave wall when, finally, the snow is fully melted. The nights remain cold but the days grow warmer.

It's a bright afternoon, the warmest yet, when Nora calls to Jude across the hot spring. "Come here, you have to see this."

He floats over to her. "What is it?"

She stays submerged. Through the steam her smiling lips entice more than any fruit Jude's ever seen. She points to the bank of the spring, where a small cluster of crocuses has emerged. They weren't there yesterday. The slender green blades must have appeared overnight and already one bears a tiny white flower.

"Beautiful, isn't it?" Nora asks.

Jude meets her eyes. "Yes, beautiful."

"Spring is coming," she says.

"I think it's already here."

"Then we should celebrate!" she says, bobbing with excitement in the water.

Jude calms his imagination. He tries to keep his eyes on the little flower. "What do you have in mind?"

"A song. Will you play for me? I could sing."

"Okay, sure." Jude shudders at his response, at the ease at which consent forms on his tongue. He realizes he would say yes to anything she asks.

"You know *La Primevera* by Vivaldi?"

"Of course. But I'll be rusty."

"You can warm up. Let's make that our song tonight."

He nods, at a loss for words. Whatever resistance he once held against her, it has melted as completely as the snow. He doesn't care that she's from the Convent. He doesn't care that she's different.

That night, when he plays *Primavera* and she sings, the universe shrinks around their cave, pressing them closer. The flames dance to their music, the light too bright for shadows. Something deep and true and powerful whispers to Jude that the sound they make together is a treasure, a magic.

38

♀

Thawing

NO MORE SNOWFLAKES FALL after *La Primavera*. The earth gives rise to countless flowers around the hillside—crocuses and daisies and buttercups. They form beds of color on the ground that was once all brown and gray and white. Nora picks flowers to decorate their little cave, hanging them beside the tally marks. The flowers will fade anyway, and so will their time here. She feels almost sad when Jude first suggests it.

"I think we're ready," he says, one late afternoon in the water of the hot spring. The sun is low, the light golden, drawing life up from the ground. "You still want to go back?"

Nora meets his intense green eyes through the steam. She has grown to like this place, and even this boy. But they can't stay here forever. He no longer stops for breath on their hikes to and from the spring. He wakes earlier and digs up spring onions and cooks soup out of the meat he catches. He plays the most exquisite violin pieces every night. She sings with him. She senses his vigor returned. His energy is too much for their cave.

"The trip will be easy now," she says. "We can reach the Convent in a couple days."

"Do you think they'll expect us?"

"No, it's been too long. They gave you only a week to bring me back. They'll think you changed your mind, or worse."

"You really think Ma and Esau will be okay?"

She nods, remembering the look on Jude's face when he first told her they'd killed his Pa. "They won't hurt them."

"If they thought I changed my mind, wouldn't they have sent others out searching for you?"

Nora's chest tightens. "I don't know. Maybe they did."

"What do you mean, *maybe?*" He swims closer, studying her.

"A helicopter passed once. They didn't stop."

"The Convent has a helicopter?"

Nora shakes her head. "I think it was from the Capital."

"That sounds bad," Jude says. "Aren't they dangerous?"

"I don't know. They protect our lands." Nora looks away. She drags her finger along the surface of the steaming water and watches the ripples spread. "They didn't see me. Or they did and ignored me. Surely they saw the smoke. That was weeks ago. No one has come. Remember, they called me contaminated."

He swims closer. "Are you?"

Her gaze rises and meets his. There's disappointment and

confusion and something more potent in the space between them. "I don't want to lose you, Jude. We could stay here a while longer."

"Really? Is that what you want?"

"I don't know what I want." Even as the words come out, she's not sure she believes them. The Convent could have found her if they'd tried. They took Jude's family. "I want to help you get your family back. Then I guess I'll stay there. It's where I belong."

He moves closer. His hand finds hers under the water. "No, not anymore."

She doesn't pull back. A ring of warm steam envelopes them. "What do you mean?"

"You belong with me."

"I can't. I—"

He puts a finger softly to her lips. "I love you, Nora."

She squeezes her eyes shut, not believing this. Then her eyes open and he's there, closer than ever before. His green eyes are bright and curious and eager.

A faint voice hisses inside her: *get away, he's dangerous, he's . . .*

No, he's Jude. He's so close.

It goes against everything she's learned. It violates the Convent's rules. It threatens risk and war. But it feels so right, so natural, and she doesn't want to stop it.

The space between them closes. Their lips touch.

Her world turns upside down.

39

♂

Returning

JUDE WATCHES NORA IN AWE. Sunlight streams into the cave's opening, basking her in light as she carves a final line into the wall. Seventy-seven marks. Eleven weeks. Jude slept for three of them, and he recovered and fell in love during the others. She could do nothing and be an angel. But she has done everything for him—kept him alive, nursed him back to health, given life new meaning—which makes her something even more beyond his reach. And yet she's here, with him, ready to leave their little cave together. *I don't deserve her*, he thinks, *but I'll try.*

"Can I use it now?" Jude holds out his hand.

Nora turns with a curious smile and puts the carving stone into his hand, her fingers grazing his.

He steps to the wall and feels Nora's gaze on him. He carefully carves a new set of lines, forming letters and words.

NORA AND JUDE

"There," he says. "It's official."

Nora laughs. "Nicely done. But I don't think anyone was competing with us for the cave."

"Not the cave." He takes her hands. "Us. Where *we* began."

She embraces him and they hold each other, letting the sun's warmth wash over them and color all their memories of the cave in a brighter hue. When she releases him and steps back, there are tears in her eyes. "Those first weeks were so hard."

"I know. Thank you for saving me."

"Thank you for giving me a reason to."

"The past weeks haven't been so bad."

"They've been wonderful." She gazes down, as if deep in thought. "There was a book at your old home, *Jane Eyre*. I read it, and I think I finally understand something Jane said to Mr. Rochester."

"What's that?"

She meets his eyes. "*All my heart is yours, sir; it belongs to you.*"

"Wow." He blushes and smiles and leans forward and kisses her. "Thank God for those bees. We might never have come here."

She laughs. "It's harder to leave than I thought."

He takes her hand and gently presses it against the newly carved letters on the rock wall. "We'll come back. It's our place now."

"I'd like that."

They leave the cave and walk down toward the lake's

edge. It's the warmest day yet. The forest bursts with life and smells of growing things. Bright green everywhere, dotted with white crocuses and yellow buttercups. Birds sing like they're at the gate of heaven.

At the shore, Jude recognizes the place where he camped with Esau and his friends so long ago, where Nora captured them. He turns and gazes back up the hillside, toward their secret hot spring. There's no visible sign of what they shared here. No hint of the cave or the hot spring, other than a few clusters of gray rocks glimpsed through the dense trees.

Jude sighs and a word slips out. "Eden."

"What?"

"That's what we should name this place."

She cocks an eyebrow. "Eden was supposed to be paradise."

"There was a hot spring!"

"Boys . . ." she shakes her head, grinning. "Always trying to name things."

Jude laughs. "I guess I better start acting more like a citizen."

"Yes." She looks him up and down. "You'll need fresh citizen clothes, too. Remember where I'll leave them?"

"In the barn behind a milk bucket."

"Good. And you remember the codes?"

"Of course. Vivaldi. If you say that when you pass, I'll know the plan's on."

"And for the buildings?"

He rolls his eyes. "We've rehearsed it a dozen times. If I

can memorize scales, don't you think I can remember a few building coordinates?"

"B minor?"

"The chicken coop building. White brick walls, two chimneys, furthest to the left from the Convent entrance."

"F sharp, then G, then B?"

"The dorm building, second to the right after entering, where most of the citizens live. Ground floor. Second door."

"Good."

Jude grins at her satisfied response. She makes a fine teacher, always pushing for clarity and perfection. He almost dreams of bringing a couple pupils into the world with her, but no, they haven't gone that far. It wouldn't be right. Not yet.

They walk together along the path Jude first took toward the Convent. They hike through the forest and up to the ridge where a fence marks the boundary. From there they can see the Convent in the distance. A white city on a hill.

Jude stops before a sign fixed on the fence. "What does it mean that this is *restricted area* and *government property*?"

"It's posted as a warning," Nora says. "To keep people out."

"I get that." Jude remembers what Ma once said about the Capital. "But is it also to keep you *in*? The Capital set this up as an experiment, right?"

"These are Convent lands, but there are broader powers that oversee our protection. The mothers handle that for us."

"So you don't know?"

She shrugs and gazes away. "No, I guess not. We never had to worry about it inside."

"I never had to worry about that stuff at my home either. Pa had his gun, and we stayed hidden. I'm not sure that's going to work anymore."

"Right. Well, today has enough trouble of its own."

"Not too much for us." Jude sounds more confident than he feels. He and Nora haven't figured out exactly what they'll do once he gets inside the Convent. If he finds Ma and Esau, he'll get out with them. Then, if nothing else, Nora will come to meet him back at the cave. It's a slender hope. It's the best they have.

They climb over the fence and move quietly through the forest.

They reach the river at dusk. It's further than they've walked in weeks, and their legs feel like lead when they finally set up camp. They eat the food they've brought cold, and sleep without a fire. It would do no good for them to be spotted now.

The next morning brings a pale orange sunrise. They set to walking just as the sun crests the horizon. Robins sing over their progress, nervous energy simmering and bubbling into a boil by the time they first glimpse the red barn.

"This is where I first saw you," Jude whispers.

"I remember. You told me your name."

Jude presses his eyes closed, still dazzled by the memory. She was an angel from the start. His real live girl.

He turns to her. "We've come a long way since then."

Her palms press against his chest, then her lips against his, and he forgets everything but this moment, amazed that she is real and not a dream.

"We're not finished yet," she says. "Let's go."

They sneak forward until they reach the edge of the grassy field. It looks the same as before. There's no sign of the mothers or any other women. The plan is on.

40

♀

Homecoming

CROSSING THE BROAD FIELD, with the Convent looming above like a celestial body, Nora thinks about the elastrator. She used the simple tool for a simple procedure. She did what she was supposed to do. She knelt in her dress as the mothers watched. The metal had only grazed the calf's groin. An inch away and none of this would have happened. But it did: the young bull spooked and ran. She chased after it and finished the job near the river. Then she saw Jude. Nothing has been the same since.

She spots the same cow with the brown flecks, now a steer. It grazes peacefully on the dewy grass. Tranquil. Docile. The Convent succeeded in its mission, but after months alone with a real, unfiltered boy, Nora doubts it's worth the cost. Jude has a spirit that the servants of the Convent never show—he can be brash and crude, sure, but his energy and drive are like nothing she's never seen.

Or maybe I'm just contaminated.

She passes two citizens pitching straw by the barn. They wear the typical brown robes of Convent citizens.

She waves. "Good morning."

They look surprised to see her, but they know better than to question a woman. They give a demure bow and wave back. They avoid meeting her eyes. Jude would never do that. He'd stare at her with his eager eyes. Part of her would feel uneasy, but part of her would be enticed. There's no enticement with these citizens. They're no longer boys. They're only servants on a long, slow march of duty.

The Convent bells strike twice in the distance. She still has some time before the morning meeting. Amazing how well she remembers the rhythm of this place, like it's a part of her.

She slips into the barn and finds a set of clothes folded on a shelf by the door. The servants always keep extras here. It would never do for them to return to the Convent dirty. She takes the clothes and spots keys hanging on a ring. She studies them quickly. She's not sure which one goes to what, and she knows the servants don't get access to everything, but they're bound to help. She takes the whole ring and hides it with the clothes behind a half-full bucket of milk. Jude will have a good start.

When she leaves the barn, she orders the citizens to escort her. They walk alongside her toward the main entrance. The bells chime again. Right on time, she'll be ready to enter the morning meeting.

She keeps her head up, confident as a mother, as she enters the Convent between the two white pillars. The familiar brick path and crisp white buildings look smaller than she remembers. They are confined, here on this hilltop by the river. The neat order of the rosebushes holds none of the allure of the wilds.

Stop, she tells herself. *Play the part.*

She turns to the servants by her side. "Citizens, you may go to your rooms now."

They exchange a glance, but nod and walk off together. Their obedience builds her confidence.

She strides forward, returning to her old way of thinking—of comfort and control here. She must truly be like a returning mother. She'll tell them about the dangers of her kidnapping, which is true enough. She'll reveal nothing of how she feels about the boy, or of what they've shared together. She'll tell them about how she struggled and fought and escaped as soon as she could. She'll tell them the boy is sick and alone in the woods.

"Nora? Nora!" Her old friend, Eve, rushes up to her. Her blue eyes are as wide as lakes in surprise. "It's really you."

"Yes, I'm back." Nora injects relief into her voice. "Will you come with me to the mothers?"

"Of course!" Eve pats the violin case by her side. "Well, it's time for me to teach, but the newbies can wait. You look . . . rough. We heard all about what happened with the boy. Did he hurt you? How did you get back? Tell me everything!"

"I'm safe now, that's what matters." Nora slips her arm into Eve's and starts to walk up the hill to the Convent. "Stay with me and I'll tell you and the mothers together. Is the morning meeting still going?"

"Yes, of course. I left a little early. But, you know, nothing really changes here. Except . . ."

"What?"

"We thought you were gone. Like, forever. And I . . ."

At Eve's hesitation, Nora realizes for the first time that her friend wears an all-white robe. She looks natural in it.

"I see," Nora says. Eve took her place.

"It's okay," Eve says. "We can make this right. Let's talk to the other mothers. We will decide what to do."

"Yes, good. Let's go there." Nora lightens her tone. She will not sound contaminated. "So how are things here?"

"Same as ever. You know, lessons and performances, meals and songs. The mothers who left to find you wouldn't say a word about what happened."

Nora finds that interesting. The mothers had failed to bring her or the boy back. They wouldn't admit that Jude had spoiled their plans and maintained control over the situation, even after they killed his father.

"It's been hard," Nora says. "And you'll hear it all. But please, it's so good to be back, won't you tell me more of what I missed? I want to hear all the little details. Who won the last performance? Are there any new little ones?"

As they walk, Eve talks. She's a fountain of information. The Convent had plenty of food during the winter. Three babies have been born. The cutest little girls. It has now been nine years since a boy was born. Eve calls it a miracle.

Nora also learns that Lilith has only a month left as the lead mother. After the failed quest to get her and Jude back, the other mothers voted on her retirement to matriarch. Not explicitly for that reason, of course. It was inevitable, with the natural clock done ticking. And it's supposed to be a high honor, but Nora knows Lilith would never want it. She could resist it. She could be dangerous—not like a male—but in her own way.

With an arm locked with Eve's, Nora enters the Great Hall like an injured war hero returning home, or so Jude might put it. She leans more on Eve and limps slightly. She smiles gracefully as more and more faces gather and stare wide-eyed at her.

She feels almost like a bride of old, except that instead of going to her bridegroom before the crowd, she strides to the twelve chairs at the front of the Hall. Twelve chairs with eleven wise faces, and one chair empty. Her chair, or Eve's.

Expressionless, the mothers watch her approach.

"Welcome back," Lilith says, as if she expected her. "Other than your attire, you look surprisingly well. What happened?"

"The boy kidnapped me," Nora says.

"We know." Lilith fingers the ruby on her necklace. "Much time has passed. How did you get back?"

Nora realizes this is no triumphant celebration of her return. It's an inquisition. "He kept me locked up, then he tried to bring me back here. He said he was going to trade me."

"Then where is he?" Lilith asks.

"In the forest, not far from here. He was stung by bees. He's allergic to them and nearly died. We have to go back for him."

"You would rescue your kidnapper?" another mother asks.

Nora glances from face to face. Under the mothers' serene masks, they seem wary. Too wary.

Contaminated. That's what they think.

Nora makes her voice harsh. "After what he did, I don't care if he dies. But shouldn't we conform all to thrive in the Convent? This one deserves no special treatment. Death would be too easy."

The mothers nod as if approving. There are hints of smiles.

"Very well," Lilith says. "Take us to him and we'll let you handle the *conforming* yourself."

"Thank you, mothers." Nora bows her head in appreciation. "We must hurry."

41

♂

B Minor

JUDE CLIMBS HIGH INTO a giant oak by the river. He gathers sticks and leaves for camouflage. He hides and waits. The morning passes. He starts to worry by afternoon.

But then he spots them in the distance. A parade of twelve women. Six wear head-to-toe white robes, marking them as mothers. The other six wear dark traveling clothes, including Nora. They move like warriors, and there are more than Nora expected. Not a good sign.

She leads the women past the barn and glides along the grassy field. If all has gone according to their plan, Nora will lead them past this tree.

She heads right at him. Jude barely breathes.

"... his mother taught him." Nora's voice carries far.

"But who else?" one of the mothers asks coldly. "We've tested her. She can't play nearly as well as he did. He must have had another teacher."

Tested her. Ma's alive. She's there.

"He learned alongside E11," Nora says. "Maybe he picked up some things from him."

"That is circular," one of them snaps. "The same woman taught them both. Your brain is clouded, child."

The group has come to the edge of the field.

Nora opens a gate in the fence, less than a stone's throw from Jude's tree. Her voice comes out meekly. "I'll admit the woods are not a place for ordered thought. But I heard the wild boy play often. He has unorthodox style yet perfect tone. He learned from the same masters whose songs we play. He knows many by heart. Bach, Tchaikovsky, Vivaldi."

Vivaldi. The plan is on.

"They hold the secrets to great music deep within their masterpieces," Nora continues. "They are unguarded, if someone has the keys to access them. Take Minuet in B minor, for example. He—"

"Yes, yes, of course," the woman interrupts as they pass beneath the tree. "But no one gains his talent by self-instruction alone. There must have been others. Enough of that. We will test him ourselves. You are sure we will reach him today?"

"Yes, it's not much farther, if we move quickly," Nora says. "You should have him play the violin concerto in A minor. His bowing is unusual, drawing out F sharps, but—"

"Tell me again, what did he . . ."

The women's voices fade as they disappear into the forest. Jude's mouth curls into a smile. Nora's message was loud and clear. She executed the plan brilliantly.

Now it's his turn. First stop: the barn.

Jude counts to one hundred before risking the climb down. The songs of birds and chatters of squirrels return once the women have left. The field ahead is tranquil.

He moves low and quiet through the grasses, mulling over Nora's words. B minor, A minor, F sharp—the buildings he must enter to find Ma and Esau. B minor is the chicken coop, just inside the gate. A minor is within the Great Hall, but somewhere beneath it, likely the sires' prison. F sharp means the sixth door, but also that that there will be guards.

Jude listens carefully as he approaches the red barn. He hears only the sounds of cows as he slips inside. Lazy dust motes show no sign of activity. It smells of animals and hay. Pitchforks lean against the wall. There are hooks with various tools.

He moves further in, scanning around the empty pails and jars. He does not see the clothes Nora said would be here. He checks the open stalls and sees a pail at the back of one.

He thinks back over Nora's words.

Deep within their masterpieces ... if someone has the keys ...

He goes to the pail and finds it half full of milk, which seems strange. Why would the servants leave it here? He lifts it, revealing a neat pile of folded clothes. The clothes are the drab brown attire of a Convent citizen. And underneath them there's a ring of keys.

She's brilliant.

He changes into the clothes and pockets the keys. Then

he walks toward the main gate with his hood up, like a normal laboring citizen of the Convent. No one pays him any mind as he enters, turns left on a brick path, and approaches building B.

It is a long and low chicken coop, with a small two-story house at one end. Ma always did take good care of her chickens. Maybe they put her to work here.

He stops outside a back door, tucked within a thick fold of ivy that climbs the wall, and hidden from the Convent behind the building. He listens carefully and hears only a faint humming song from upstairs in the building.

The handle is unlocked. He moves silently inside.

The room smells of Ma. Her favorite herb, lavender, hangs above a small table and single chair. There's a pot over the fire, slowly cooking broth with onions and garlic. He's in the right place.

Creeping on tiptoes he moves to the slender stairs in the corner. He again hears the faint hummed tune. It stops him cold.

It's Ma's voice, and she hums an old lullaby she used to sing when Jude was scared at night. It's so out of place that it sounds like a warning. He creeps back outside and tries to get a glimpse inside the second-story window. He pushes a nearby cart to the wall and slowly draws himself up by gripping the window ledge. He peeks inside and sees two women standing guard by Ma's sides.

He climbs down and thinks. If her humming is truly meant to warn him, then she must have seen him approach, or heard him enter. He can signal to her somehow.

He purses his lips and calls out in a bird song. Three notes only: B, A, C. Again, B, A, C. Bac—back. He repeats the call irregularly a few times, then stops and waits. He hears Ma speak from the window. Her voice is muffled. But soon she is going downstairs, checking the pot over the fire.

She takes a spoon and lifts it to her lips. As she sips, she glances out the back window and their eyes connect. Her sad eyes show no shock, only fear. She shakes her head vigorously as if trying to warn him away.

"What is it?" a woman's hard voice asks.

"The soup's no good," Ma says. "Too watery. Needs more broth. I know just the chicken to add."

"No," the woman replies. "Orders are for you to stay in here until the search party returns."

"You want tepid soup?" Ma asks.

"Well, if it's just one chicken . . ." another woman says. "It'll be fine. I'll go with her."

The other woman grunts approval, and moments later Ma and a stern-looking woman, wide as a barrel, step out of the small brick house. Jude watches them from behind the cart. They slip into the low chicken coop, and he follows after them.

Ma chats lightly with the guard behind her as they make their way down the rows of cages. Their talk and the soft straw on the floor muffle Jude's steps.

". . . And so sometimes ya gotta grab it by the throat," Ma says.

Jude figures it's a hint. He charges at the guard.

The large woman moves faster than he expected. She twists away from him, and within two seconds she has him flat on his back, pinned to the ground.

Ma swings the flat side of her cleaver down on the woman's head. The woman rolls off Jude, motionless and breathing shallowly.

"Jude," Ma whispers, clasping his cheeks.

"Ma."

42

♀

Distraction

"HE'S GONE," NORA SAYS, with all the shock she can muster. The place where she and Jude camped the night before is, of course, empty. "He was right here. He was . . ."

"Near death, you said." The mother glares down at Nora, arms crossed. "Looks like he recovered fast."

Nora's gaze falls from the mother's long white robe to her big black boots, covered in mud. It's the first time a mother has made her sick to her stomach. Mothers who are supposed to lead the Convent in life and love and gentleness. This one looks ready to squash Nora like a bug under her boot.

"It's impossible," Nora mutters. "He could barely move after he was stung. I swear."

The mother's face is stern. "Those who swear are those who dare too much."

"We have to search for him. He must be close."

"I will decide that." The mother looks to the other

women. "Do you smell smoke? Could he have built a fire?"

"No sign of a fire, but it rained yesterday," another woman says. "The forest is too dense here to see far."

"Stella, Min, search for any trace of heat."

The two women, clad in black, pull down their headsets and inspect the surroundings. They start at the place Nora identified and sweep around from there. Nora knows they'll find no heat. She knew it would get delicate from here, but she expected more trust than the mother has shown. Time is running short.

Stella returns with her headset pulled off and dangling from her hand like a set of large insect eyes. "Nothing. No one has been here in a day."

All eyes turn to Nora. She stays calm, changes tack. "I wonder . . ." she puts a finger to her lips, as if deep in thought.

"Yes?" the mother says.

"He had me tied up. He could have been trying to trick us, to let me escape and come to you and see what we'd do. But he really did look sick. He was pale and clammy. He couldn't have been faking that."

The mother steps closer. She stares at Nora as if peering into her soul. "What are you hiding?"

Nora lets a hint of guilt creep over her posture, shoulders slump, gaze down. Her voice comes out soft and sincere. "When I was locked up, before, in a cellar under their family's cabin, there were books. I had nothing to do. I read them."

"What books?"

"A lot of old ones. Jane Eyre, parts of the Bible."

The mother narrows her eyes. "And?"

"I'm sorry, but I'm confused now. I have questions about things. About the world outside the Convent."

"Of course you do. You're not a fool. You were once chosen as a mother. If the boy hadn't taken you, you'd be reading and thinking and talking with us, as all mothers do. We have the answers." The mother clasps Nora's shoulder. "Boys like this one are very dangerous. I can see his taint on you. We'll bring you back and help you heal. He'll be the last boy you have to deal with."

"Thank you," Nora says.

"Mother, mother!" A woman rushes up from the forest. Panic fills her face. "The Convent is on fire!"

She runs off and the group of women races after her. They reach a rocky outcrop by the river, with a view of the Convent in the distance. Dark billows of smoke rise in the clear blue sky.

43

♂

Sanctum

JUDE STRUCK THE FLAME in the chicken coop. The spark spread to straw and wood and dung, into a roaring blaze.

It was Ma's idea. Jude had told her quickly what happened and how he got there. He didn't mention Pa, not yet. They had to save Esau. Ma said they needed a distraction so they could search for him. They dragged the unconscious guard out of the coop and opened the doors to let the chickens fly out with a flurry of feathers. Ma led Jude away and toward the Great Hall, like a normal woman of the Convent followed by a servant.

Now the fire rages behind them. Flames flicker along the roof of the coop. Smoke billows black and pungent. The buildings close by will catch soon if the flames are left unchecked. Women race downhill past Jude and Ma, hurrying to the fire.

"The hoses!" a woman shouts. "More hoses!"

Ma keeps her head down and moves urgently. She says not a word as she approaches the Great Hall. Jude follows her lead. He wonders about Nora. They will have found that he's gone by now. Will they believe Nora? Will they punish her? Maybe they are bringing her back even now. His gut twists at the thought of leaving this place without her. Saving Ma and Esau isn't worth losing Nora. He has to save all three.

Ma leads the way inside the Hall, through the main doors. The vast room is mostly empty, with only a few women sitting in pews. An older woman near the back turns and her gaze lingers on Ma, eyes widening.

Ma takes a deep breath, as if remembering something. "Fire!" she yells. "Everyone to the coop. Now!"

The women start to rise but Ma doesn't wait. She turns quickly toward a staircase going up.

"The lead mother is usually up here," Ma whispers between breaths. "There's a secured entry to the sires. It's our best chance of finding Esau."

A minor. F sharp, Nora said. But Ma already seems to know where they are going. Jude can't help but ask: "Why didn't you tell me you were a mother?"

Ma turns to him. Her eyes carry weathered sadness. "To protect you, Jude. I will tell you more later. We must hurry. When I say 'now,' you close the door and help me, okay?"

Jude nods.

"They won't expect us to use force. They never do." Ma leads them up the stairs to a long, red-carpeted hall. She strides forward, passing many doors, with the confidence of someone who has taken a path countless times before.

They reach an open door at the end of the hallway. Jude thinks they must be near the back corner of the Great Hall building. Inside, a young woman in a white robe sits at a desk. She has dark ringlets and large brown eyes. Her hands are folded before her, with a practiced calm.

"Is Lilith here?" Ma asks, closing the door behind her.

The young woman looks Ma up and down. "Do I know you?"

"No, I've been away a long time," Ma says. "I've returned with an urgent message."

The woman's gaze passes briefly over Jude, as if acknowledging the presence of a mule. "Do you have an appointment?"

"It's an emergency." Ma rushes forward and leans over the desk. "There's a fire in the Convent."

"The lead mother knows of the fire." The woman's only movement is a blink of her eyes. "Who sent you?"

"Krystal."

The woman stiffens. "But she's . . ."

Ma is already around the side of the desk, and a flash of metal comes to the woman's neck. The point of a dagger is there, touching skin.

"She's dead," Ma says. "And you will be too if you don't cooperate."

The woman doesn't budge. She has the look of a child who has, for the first and last time, put a hand on a burning stove. "What do you want?"

"The keys." Ma holds out her free hand.

The woman reaches cautiously toward the desk.

"No," Ma demands, pressing the dagger point against flesh. "Step away from the desk. Slowly now."

The woman does as she's told.

"Give me the keys in your pocket. I know they're there."

"How do you . . . ?"

"Now."

The woman pulls out a ring with two keys from a pocket hidden within her white robe. Ma takes the key ring and tosses it to Jude. "Lock the hallway door."

Jude does it quickly. Then he and Ma gag the woman and tie her hands and feet together behind her back. It takes only a minute. They've had practice with goats that are far less compliant.

Ma goes to the door at the back of the room. She opens it with the other key. The next room is stunning. High ceilings, walls lined with bookshelves, and ornate furnishings.

A woman stands at the center, facing them, as if she knew they were coming. Jude recognizes her as the one who jabbed a needle into Pa, who killed him. Her white robe and close-cut hair give her the look of a monk. Her cold, indignant eyes give her the look of a queen.

"Welcome, Genevieve."

"Hello, Lilith. You've risen far."

"Almost as far as you've fallen."

Ma steps forward with her dagger raised. "You know why

I'm here."

The woman stands her ground, like an oak in a breeze. "To be honest, my old friend, I'm not so sure. Is your plan to kill me? Like you did to Krystal? Perhaps as vengeance for your dear J2? Or do you plan to tie me up like you did to poor Eve out there?"

"That depends," Ma says. "If you let me leave with my boys, I will let you live."

Lilith holds out her palms, as if in a peace offering. "You may take E11. Its seed was no good."

"So he's already . . . ?"

"Yes, we've given him peace."

"Then why do you keep him here, with the sires?"

"As a kindness to him. He has not yet adjusted."

"Take me to him."

Lilith nods graciously. She glides to one of the high bookshelves and reaches for a book. As she pulls it, there's a faint metallic click. The entire shelf suddenly swings back.

"Lead the way," Ma says, still gripping the dagger.

Lilith moves through the doorway, followed by Ma, then Jude. The hidden passage leads to an austere corridor that he recognizes from his last infiltration of the Convent. The floors and walls and ceiling are dull concrete. A dozen metal doors line the way.

The woman and Ma stop before a door with the number "6" affixed to the wall outside.

"Open it," Ma demands.

Lilith smiles in condescension, as if she maintains

complete control over the situation. "You never had the patience to rule as a mother."

"And you never had the love. Open it."

Lilith leans toward a small screen below the number 6. A green light flashes, and like magic, the door slides open.

44

♀

Flames

PANIC SWIRLS IN THE CONVENT streets. Two buildings are ablaze. One has already roasted down to stumps. Smoke clouds everything and stings Nora's eyes.

Please, Mother God, let no one be hurt.

She feels a tinge of guilt. Did Jude start this? Did she unleash it? It's worse than she imagined. She never expected a fire, destruction. This is still her home.

"Lucy, Stella, Min, over there!" The mother beside Nora barks out the orders. She points to a line of women hauling buckets of water, then to the opposite side of the Convent, where another group of women is dousing sparks that attempt to jump from one barracks to another. The three women charge off.

"The rest of you, with me!" The mother motions for Nora to follow up the hill.

She hurries after them toward the Great Hall. It shows no

sign of flame or smoke. Two women dressed in black stand on guard by the doors. Nora has never seen such precautions. The guards bow and step aside as the mother leads them in.

The Great Hall has none of the turmoil outside, but nervous faces turn to them as they enter. Another mother, Selene, approaches their group with her hair bun bobbing. She exchanges quiet words with the mother who escorted Nora. All Nora overhears is, *"He wasn't there."*

Selene glares at Nora. "Come with me," she orders. "You two, join us." She points to two black-clad women who look like sisters, with olive complexion and serious eyes.

Selene leads the small group up to a long hallway, where Nora knows the lead mother, Lilith, will be. The door at the end of the hallway is closed. She has never seen it closed.

Selene pulls at the handle. "Locked," she mutters. She slides a discrete white panel on the white wall, revealing a set of lights and buttons. Two of them flash red.

She turns urgently to the two guards. "Go, gather all the mothers in the Hall. Tell them it is a Code T."

The guards nod and race off.

Selene faces Nora. "You will stay with me."

"Code T?" Nora asks.

"I fear you will soon see," she says. "The lead mother is always available to the Convent. If she has sealed this door, then she is in danger. And if you have caused this . . ." Her face darkens.

"I've been with the others. I haven't done anything. I—"

"*You* are contaminated. And now you will follow me. In

silence." Selene turns with a twirl of white robe and leans close to the panel of buttons beside the door.

A small button, like a doorbell, blinks green. The door swings open, and Selene rushes in.

The waiting room is empty and quiet.

Selene gasps as she approaches another door at the back. Her eyes are on the floor. Nora catches up and sees a body, a mother, tied up. Eve's familiar doe-brown eyes meet Nora's.

Selene kneels and unties the gag over her mouth.

"They came," Eve blurts out, "and I couldn't, and—"

"Slow down," Selene says as she unties the other ropes at Eve's ankles and wrists. "One thing at a time. Who did this?"

"There were two of them." Eve stands and stretches. "An older woman and a young citizen."

"What did they say?"

"The woman wanted to see the lead mother. I said she was not available and suddenly the woman drew a knife. It all happened so fast. They took my keys and tied me up."

"Then what?" Selene asks.

"They went into the lead mother's office. There was nothing I could do. I'm so sorry. I've never—"

"What did the woman look like?"

"Long black hair, streaks of gray. She was . . . pretty."

Selene nods knowingly. "And the citizen?"

"I didn't get a good look. It had its hood up."

"Any beard?"

Eve shakes her head, but then pauses. "Maybe whiskers."

"The boy." Selene turns to Nora with a glare so intense

that Nora steps back.

"What's happening?" Eve asks. "Who were they?"

Before anyone can answer, a new alarm sounds. This is the loudest yet, like an emergency siren welling up from within the Convent.

Selene rushes to the desk and rummages through a drawer. She pulls out a gun. "Stand by that wall," she orders Nora and Eve.

As they move to obey, Eve takes Nora's hand and presses close. The mother stands before them, facing the door behind the desk, with her gun leveled.

45

♂

Brother

JUDE FOLLOWS MA AND LILITH into the room. After the austere hallway of metal doors, he expects a prison and instead finds luxury. An ornate rug covers the floor, and a bright fire burns in a hearth. There's a smell of fragrant oils. It's like the room where Nora took him months ago.

In the center, a person reclines in a leather chair, watching a video on a screen. The video shows water flowing over a rock in a stream, over and over, tranquil and mesmerizing.

"You have guests," Lilith says.

The person rises slowly, almost reluctantly, in drab brown clothes. One turn of the head and Jude knows: it's Esau.

Ma rushes to him and sweeps him up in her arms. He stands a head taller, body stiff and awkward. He sees Jude and, when their eyes meet, Jude sinks. The fire that once blazed in his brother, crude as it was, has faded. Listlessness hangs over him. His cheeks are soft and smooth. His body looks lethargic.

Ma steps back and sizes him up. "We're going to set you free."

"Free?" Esau's shoulders slump like a boy who dropped his ice cream. "But I like it here."

Ma spins to Lilith. "You drugged him. We were never to do that unless the Convent is in danger."

Lilith smiles at Esau like a doting mother. "Yes, precisely."

"What are you trying to say?" Ma asks.

"I don't think you want to know."

"Tell me."

Lilith sighs. "We tested him like any other. His T was off the charts. Boys like him, allowed to become men, are the reason we're here, Genevieve. He's a fighter, a war-starter, a Lamech. We're doing what we can to help him find peace."

"I don't believe you," Ma says. "You knew I'd come. He's a hostage."

"Come now, old friend, why accuse me? You are the one who ran away. I'm the one who allowed it."

Ma's jaw clenches. She glances to Jude with the same look she gave when she told him to escape through the cellar of their cabin, like a mother bear ready to protect her cubs. She turns back to Lilith and says: "Show me his biometrics. Now."

For the first time, a flash of surprise passes over Lilith, replaced quickly by a masked grin. "Very well. Your children will stay here."

Ma points her dagger at Lilith. "If you try anything, I will do what I must."

"Oh, I don't doubt that. You're the one who left the Convent with a violent man, remember?"

Ma scowls but replies simply, "Let's go."

Lilith bows her head to Jude and Esau. "I hope you enjoy your little reunion."

She turns to leave. Ma follows after her. As she passes Jude, she brushes against him and slips two keys into his hand. "*Exire*," she whispers.

Get out, in Latin.

The door closes behind the women, sealing Jude and Esau inside.

"Hi Jude," Esau says. "Ya like my place here?"

Jude meets Esau's eyes and swallows at the emptiness there. "What did they do to you?"

"Who? The mothers? They're so nice. They found the sickness inside me and they took it out. I'm doing better now. They give me medicine and nice things to eat and drink and watch. I'm happy here. I'm glad ya came to visit."

"I'm going to make this better," Jude says.

Esau grins and starts to hum: "Ya have to admit it's getting better, a little better all the time . . ."

Jude sighs and glances around. He has to find a way out. He goes to the door and confirms it's locked. There's not even a handle. The keys Ma gave him will be no use, not here. He remembers the panel beside the door on the outside, but inside there is no panel. He slams his shoulder into the door a couple times. It produces only pain.

"Whatcha doin'?" Esau asks.

Jude stares at his brother. "Do you know a way out?"

"No reason to leave, but . . ." Esau holds up the screen in his hand, like a kid showing off a lollipop. "If I need help, I can just push the buttons on this."

"Show me."

Esau shuffles closer and taps against the screen a few times. Jude has never seen anything like it. Esau navigates through it easily, as if well familiar with the menu of buttons. He quickly comes to one called *Help*, and he taps it. Nothing happens.

"What now?" Jude asks.

"Some nice lady comes to help. I figure they'll bring more medicine soon anyway."

"How often do they come? And how long does it take?"

"A while. Time don't matter much here."

Jude cringes. He imagines Pa locked in a room like this, drugged and dwindling away for years. He has a feeling the "help" button isn't going to do much, especially when there's a fire in the Convent and the lead mother and her assistant are out of commission.

He paces to the glass wall on the far side of the room. The view of the waterfall is nearly the same as the room he visited with Nora months ago, when he leapt off with her into the river.

He looks back at Esau. "Can you open the window?"

"Nope. Why would I want to?"

Jude shakes his head. His brother is not going to be much help. And leaping into the river isn't going to save Ma or stop the Convent or reunite him with Nora. He needs another option.

He goes back to searching the room and inspects a small, doorless alcove with a toilet. Above, on the ceiling, there's an air duct. It looks just large enough to fit him, even Esau. But metal bolts fix it tightly in place.

He drags in a standing lamp with gilded, golden curves like flowers at the base. Standing on the toilet, he slams the lamp into the air duct. It clangs loudly, but hardly makes a dent.

"Jude?"

He turns to see Esau staring at him, mouth gaping.

"Ya can't . . . do that," Esau stammers. "The nice ladies say don't break nothin'."

Jude studies his stupefied brother and an idea hits him. If the mothers drug the captives and treat them like children, then he can pretend to play along. "Haven't you wondered why they brought me here?" Jude says. "It's a game. They *want* us to try to get out. Now, get over here and help. You're taller and stronger. I bet you can knock this vent loose, if you try."

Esau hesitates, confused, and then a grin spreads over his face. "A game. Sure!"

He pads over and takes the lamp. Standing on the toilet, it takes him only three hard bashes to break a hole into the vent. When he hands the bent lamp back to Jude, his grip is tight. His expression has more of an edge. "That felt . . . different," he says.

"Good," Jude says. "How long since you last took the medicine?"

"A while, like I said."

"Okay, fine." Jude points to the large chair where Esau sat before. "Help me with that."

The brothers together drag the chair and hoist it onto the toilet. They climb up it like a ladder and pull themselves into the vent.

They crawl through the tight passage toward the main hallway. Jude stops at the next vent. He can see the hallway just below them. No one is in sight. Jude bangs against the vent and feels it start to break. It's easier to knock loose from inside. Jude slams into it again and this time it gives way. But the moment the vent drops to the ground, he starts to drop with it, head first toward the concrete.

Until he is stopped. A hand catches his ankle.

He looks up and sees Esau smiling at him.

"Got ya." Esau lowers him safely to the ground and comes after him, landing smoothly. His brother doesn't look lethargic now.

Jude glances up and down the hallway. The doorway they entered is still open, revealing the lead mother's office beyond. He doubts Ma went that way. The opposite end of the hallway has a door and a control panel.

He approaches the panel. There is a black screen, and it does nothing when he taps it. Above it, however, there's a red lever. And there's only one thing to do when confronted with a red lever.

Jude pulls it.

Every door along the hallway suddenly swings open with a metallic swoosh. Then alarms erupt, loud and wailing sirens all around.

"Whew boy!" Esau shouts, pressing his hands over his ears. "Ya still think this is a game?"

Jude's not sure of anything now. The door beside the panel is still locked shut. The women will come soon. Beside him, a tired-looking man emerges from a room. He wears a purple silk robe with a flower pattern. His thick beard and hair are in disarray.

Then another man emerges further down the hall, and another. They all look similar, wearing their robes and moving with the energy of sloths. They glance around in complete confusion, hands over their ears, but without a hint of urgency.

"Run!" Jude shouts, pointing at the far room. "Fire! Get out!"

The men hear him, and they do as he says. Not fast, not panicked, but obediently they jog toward the lead mother's office. Jude grabs Esau's hand as he moves to follow.

"Not you," he says. "Come here."

He pulls Esau with him and hides behind the open door of the last room, where one of the sires was kept. Someone is bound to come to investigate. And when they do, Jude will be ready.

46

♀

Capital

NORA WATCHES IN DISBELIEF as a bearded man appears in the doorway. Selene points her gun points at his chest. She shouts over the blaring alarm: "What happened?"

His hands go up innocently. His silken purple sleeves fall to his shoulders. "The door opened."

"Who opened it?" Selene demands.

The sire shrugs. "I don't know."

Another sire appears behind him, then another. They look as surprised as Nora. Selene orders them inside, with her gun shifting from one to another. She questions them but learns nothing except that the alarm went off and all the doors opened and someone told them to come here, so they did. They all look like they just woke up from naps.

"All of you, sit down and stay here," Selene orders.

The sires sit like obedient dogs.

"You two," Selene says to Nora and Eve. "Follow me."

Nora and Eve exchange a glance, both still confused, and then do as Selene ordered. They follow her quickly through the lead mother's office and down the sire's hallway. Like the sires said, every door is open, revealing empty rooms. Nora glances into them as they pass and sees no one.

They come to a sealed door. Selene leans close to the panel, where a light flashes green and the door opens. She steps to Eve and whispers something that Nora is clearly not supposed to hear.

"I will put things in order up here," Selene says. "Nora, do as Eve says if you want any chance of being restored as a mother."

"Yes, mother." Nora bows.

Selene storms away, back toward the lead mother's office and the sires.

Eve clasps Nora's shoulder. "I can't wait to show you this."

Nora studies her friend and sees no hint of danger, no threat of betrayal, only wonder. "What is it?"

"The heart of the Convent. You'll see. Let's go."

Eve leads them through the doorway and down a long set of stairs. They descend deep underground, so far that the alarm sound fades. The stairs end in a short hallway like the sire's hall above. Nora follows Eve through an open door at the end of the hall.

The immense room stops Nora cold.

A dozen screens line the far wall, showing live video of the Convent. Wires run along the ceilings and connect to other stations in the room. Lights flicker. Devices beep. The room pulses with energy. Nothing about it is natural.

If this is the Convent's heart, then now she knows: the Convent is built on a lie. She always believed the heart of the Convent was the Great Hall. That's where the citizens gather, the women perform, and the mothers reign. The light-filled sanctuary was always Nora's safe place in her mind. A place of peaceful order carved out of nature. A place where fears subsided.

But Nora was wrong.

"Amazing, right?" Eve says. "It's too bad you had to learn about it this way. The mothers showed me soon after I was promoted. They introduce these marvels gradually. But Selene says this is an emergency. Come on."

They are halfway across the room when Nora hears voices ahead. One is the lead mother, gray hair cut close, eyes deep and dark as a ravine. Lilith. The other woman has a wild mop of dark hair and crow's feet wrinkles at her intense eyes. Nora recognizes her from a picture: she is Jude's Ma.

Lilith strides quickly to them. She confronts Eve. "Why did you bring *her* here?"

"Selene sent her with me," Eve says. "She gave me a message."

"Well, out with it."

"The boy was not there in the forest. We saw the fire and came quickly. Then someone released the sires. Selene is returning them to their pens. She went to investigate how they were released, but didn't see any cause, so she sent me down here. Nora's a threat now. She hasn't been telling us the truth."

"Eve!" Nora gasps. "Why would you say that?!"

"*I* am a mother," her former friend says.

"Yes, I see." Lilith studies Nora briefly. "It's a shame to see you contaminated. You had such promise."

"We don't have time for this, Lilith." Jude's mother holds a blade up. "Show me."

Lilith looks from face to face. A severe grin touches her lips, sharp as a sickle. "Eve, bring up E11's data, along with Nora's."

"Yes, mother." Eve turns to the dashboard. Her fingers begin striking a pad of buttons. Nora sees letters appear on the screen before her. She's read of this but never imagined the Convent used such technology.

The screen fills with information. At the side is a picture of Jude's brother, E11. Nora learned songs from him. The mothers decided he could not be a sire. On the screen there's a large red box around several words and figures.

"You see," Lilith says. "T like this is unmanageable, as you know. And now hers?"

The information on the screen splits, with another set of data appearing, this time below Nora's picture.

"Very fine genes," Lilith says, turning to Nora. "We thought you had the makings of a lead mother. We thought you could lead the Convent into its perfect future, one in which no boys are born and no boys are needed. We've gone nine years without a baby of their kind, and we could go infinite more, until you ran off with this wild boy from outside."

"He *kidnapped* me," Nora protests. She knows it's no use arguing. She can tell Lilith has already made up her mind. But she needs time, to think, to get out.

Lilith snorts as if amused. "However it started, we can see that you have changed. It's our job as mothers to know when sheep have left the fold."

"I'm sorry you're contaminated," Eve says. "This is what boys do. If left untreated, they spread their sickness to females around them. Better to be rid of them completely."

"That's a lie," says Jude's mom.

"And you were cast out for the same reason," Lilith says. "Enough of this. Eve, inform the Capital of the fire. I'll show Genevieve the truth about her son."

Eve moves to a station and picks up a phone. "Hello, this is Eve. We have a situation. There's been . . ."

"Come on, you should see this, too." Lilith pulls Nora away from Eve and toward the wall of screens.

Nora stares in amazement at the videos. They look live, from many vantages around the Convent. Women fight the fire in the chicken coop. Others tend those with burns. More of them have gathered in the Great Hall. There are also live feeds of the sire's open rooms. And, in one of them, she sees two figures, Jude and his brother, waiting in the doorway.

No, she thinks. *Get out, get out!*

"We monitor to keep everyone safe," Lilith says. "But this is only the tip of the iceberg. Our security goes to the very roots of our citizens. Here you can see a threat. You would recognize his face. It's the wild boy who corrupted you."

The screen fills with a mesmerizing shape—two lines coiling up and down, with shorter lines connecting them, like a twisting ladder.

"This DNA shows promise," Lilith says. "Talent, yes. Health, intelligence. But look at this sequence."

The screen zooms onto a particular portion of the helix, where a series of letters appears.

"I don't expect you to understand the genetics," Lilith turns from Nora. "But Genevieve will understand."

Jude's mother looks grim. "How did you get his DNA?"

"From him, of course. He came to the Convent and took Nora. He left a few hairs behind."

"But you can't predict his children," Jude's mother says. "You can't control his offspring."

"Precisely," Lilith says. "You see, Nora, we have carefully selected and crafted the children of the mothers to ensure that no more males are born. It is far better than simply neutralizing those who are."

Nora gazes at the helix in wonder. *No more males.*

"But . . . that's . . ." With no sires, there will be no children . . .

"That's paradise," Lilith says. "You wonder how we will propagate, and the answer is simple. We have harvested and stored enough seed to last a millennium. We have set ourselves free from the sin that stains the world."

Nora keeps her face blank as she stares at the screen. She

thinks of how she felt with Jude, as he tried to protect her, as she cared for him, as he played music for her, as he kissed her, as she kissed him, and she knows: they have to stop this. For all the women here. For the unborn boys. For love.

Eve approaches from the other side of the room. "The Capital agrees with our plan, given the circumstances."

"Good," Lilith says. "Do it now. Quick and painless."

"Of course." Eve moves to a keypad and navigates through a series of selections.

Sires.

Gas.

"No!" Nora shouts. "You can't!"

"But we must," Lilith says. "The Capital agrees."

Jude's mom moves in a sudden blur. A dagger appears at Eve's neck. "Step away from the computer. Now."

"No, please," Eve begs, but doesn't move.

Lilith laughs in a quiet, cold cackle. She has a gun leveled at Jude's mom. "You really think you can stop us?"

"I won't let you kill them."

"Your sons are stained," Lilith says. "I'm sorry, old friend, but it's for the good of the Convent."

Jude's mom doesn't answer and doesn't back down. There's a sudden stillness that raises Nora's hair, like the instant before a lightning bolt. Lilith's gun points at Jude's mom, whose dagger is at Eve's neck, while Eve's fingers hover over a command that would kill the sires. One wrong move could set off everything.

Nora's eyes flick away from the deadly triangle of women

and toward the screens. The helix has been replaced by the video feeds. One of them shows the room where Jude and his brother were just minutes ago.

It's empty.

47

♂

Sacrifice

JUDE PRESSES HIS BACK TO the wall, breathing heavily. He peers around the corner again. His mind tries to process what he sees, but it's like looking into an alternate reality, a dream. There are blinking lights, glowing panels, metal devices, and four women. Two of them he wants to save, and the other two want him dead.

Esau tugs at his sleeve. "What do ya see?"

Jude turns back with his finger to his lips. "Quiet. They're in there."

"Who?"

"Ma, Nora, and two of the mothers." Jude studies his brother, who seems to have some of his fire back after escaping from the sire's quarters. Maybe the drugs are wearing off, too. "We're going to help Ma, but we'll need a way out. Any ideas?"

"Hm . . ." Esau glances around. "There's a balcony overlooking the waterfall. After the mothers took the sickness out of me, they let me sit out there and have lemonade."

"What sickness?" Jude asks.

"Somethin' called T. Oh, don't look so worried. I was scared at first, too. But they've removed it all, and I don't feel so bad."

Jude shakes his head, sick to his stomach. "Where's the balcony?"

Esau points up. "It's back upstairs."

Jude remembers the place where he leapt away with Nora. It's an option, but not a good one. He scans the short concrete hallway. There's one other door at the end. He hurries to it and tries the keys Ma gave him, just in case.

The door rises and reveals a dark tunnel going even deeper underground. He can't see how far it goes.

"Whoa," Esau says beside him.

Jude senses time running short. He can't investigate this but, wherever it leads, it's another option.

He returns to the doorway of the huge room, with Esau following close. This time when Jude glances inside, there are weapons drawn.

"Esau," he whispers.

"Yeah?"

"In the room there's a wall with a lot of buttons."

"Okay."

"I want you to run in there yelling, and get to that wall as fast as you can."

"Yellin'? But ya told me to be quiet."

"We need a distraction. I'll sneak in after you and try to

help."

"And then what?"

"Ma will know what to do."

"So ya want me to just run in yellin'?"

Jude nods. "All the way to the far wall. Like a race."

"I always beat ya in races."

"I know," Jude says. "You're perfect for this."

Esau stands a bit straighter. "If it helps Ma, I'll do it."

"Thanks, brother." Jude clasps his shoulders and wonders how on earth they've come to this. "Now, on three." He keeps his voice quiet. "One, two, *three.*"

Esau does exactly as Jude hoped. He charges into the room without a trace of hesitation. He races forward at full speed and full volume, screaming like a maniac. The women's heads lock onto him, their eyes wide in utter shock.

Jude crouches and slips in, keeping a line of metallic devices between the women and him. He creeps along the row, getting closer. The end of the row is only ten feet from the women.

"Look who's come, Genevieve." Lilith shifts the aim of her gun from Ma to Esau. "Step back from Eve. Now."

Ma presses her eyes closed, then lowers her dagger and does as Lilith says. "Esau," she sighs. "Are you okay?"

"Yeah, Ma." He stops and catches his breath. "What are y'all doing in here?"

"Trying to save you," Ma says.

"Trying to save the whole Convent," Lilith counters, smiling as her finger tenses on the trigger. "And now this will—"

Jude charges at her like a bull. He tackles her as hard as he can.

Lilith grunts and they both go down. The gun clatters on the concrete floor. She tries to scramble after it. He pulls her back. She wrestles against him, wiry and stronger than he thought, but still no match for him.

He gets the upper hand and lands a knee to her side.

"No, no!" Ma is shouting.

Jude pops up and sees a gun leveled at his chest. Eve's arm trembles, but her face is resolute. He holds up his hands and takes a step back. "Wait—"

"Do it," Lilith growls.

"No, don't," Nora whispers, stepping closer to Eve. "Please. Remember, a world of peace."

Jude searches Eve's eyes for any chance of mercy, but all he sees is solemn duty. He turns to Lilith. "I didn't hurt her."

Lilith's lips curl up into a snarl. "But you will. Men always will. You can't help yourselves, so we help you, until *wars and fightings cease.*" She looks to Eve. "End this. Now!"

The gun steadies. Jude sees a reflection of his death in Eve's doe eyes. She pulls the trigger.

There's a blur and a bang and Jude knows he's dead.

But.

A sharp stab at his shoulder.

A body falls in front of him.

God, no. It's Esau.

Jude collapses to his knees and leans over his brother. A dark pool spreads beneath him. He groans.

Jude's shoulder burns. His mind clouds. But his heart breaks. "Esau. I'm here."

His brother's dark, innocent eyes look up at him. His voice comes out as a faint gurgle. "I . . . I done it for you."

48

♀

Daughter

NORA'S HANDS INSTINCTIVELY COVER her ears. The gunshot echoes in the metallic room. Jude and his brother are down. Blood on the floor. Nora lunges toward them, but—

Jude's mom springs at Eve beside her. A dagger flashes.

Eve screams in pain. The gun falls and skitters away.

Nora knows she must get it first, much as she hates it.

As she rushes forward, Lilith charges at Jude's mom. They collide and fall and struggle on the floor. They slam into a metallic cabinet, knocking it over. It crashes onto Jude and his brother before Nora can get to them.

No. She kneels and picks up the gun. It's small and black, but heavy as death in her hand. She turns quickly, only to see Lilith swinging a blade.

"No!" Nora shouts.

And she shoots.

The bang is like a thunderclap.

Lilith rises with a bloody blade in her hand. "You missed."

She spins to the computer panel and begins typing. Two bodies lie at her feet. Eve and Jude's mom.

Create a world of peace.

It's all a lie. Was it always a lie?

"I won't miss again." Nora grips the gun with both hands, steadying it, forcing herself to believe it.

Lilith looks back and meets Nora's eyes. Her fingers poise over the keyboard. "If you shoot, the sires will die. All of them. Put the gun down, Nora."

"No. I don't believe you."

"Come now, you've seen what these two boys have done. You see the violence they let loose."

"I've seen *your* violence."

"Only in self-defense." Lilith sounds calm and composed. "We must never deny our own strength. But our greatest strength is stopping violence before it starts."

"By killing?"

"Of course not. We simply tame the evil that stains nature."

Nora considers her words, weighing their falsehood, twisting reality. She eyes the screens and controls. "Show me what you were going to show Jude's mom."

Lilith smiles as she shifts to another set of controls. "Your curiosity always served you well, until this boy contaminated you. You should have seen this already, as a new mother. It's time you learned the truth." She strikes a few keys and a screen appears with a list of names. A pointer glides to "Nora" and

Lilith clicks.

Nora expects to see her face and information. Instead, there is only a series of letters that make no sense together. AGGFFAFFG.

"What is this?" she asks.

"Your genes," Lilith says. "There is a careful process for every new life that comes to the Convent. You know our code. We seek peace. In the Convent's early years, the mothers tried to weed out the violent and the unstable. Those born with high T—the ones some call 'boys'—were particularly prone to those dangers. The mothers found a way to pacify them after birth, removing the source of the vile hormone, as you know. But that was never enough. We have tested and experimented. We have refined our insemination process until we could eliminate those with high T completely. This one who kidnapped you was the last. Never again will we allow such danger to be born in our lands."

Nora eyes the series of letters and considers Lilith's words. She's saying Jude would be the last one. No more boys. No more war, but no more of what she and Jude have shared.

"We knew you were one of the finest specimens from the start," Lilith continues. "We designed you to be."

"*Designed*?"

Lilith gazes at the screen and sighs proudly, like an artist admiring her own masterpiece. "You started from *my* egg, and I bore you, but I knew well my own flaws. We corrected those. And we curated only the best aspects of the sire's seed. Intelligent. Cautious. But also proud and loyal."

"You're my . . . ?"

"Mother, yes. But we mothers are one, you know. We practice the art of childbearing together. We hold the secrets of gene selection and pregnancy. You may still be forgiven. You may still be a mother, Nora."

The gun trembles in Nora's hands. "This . . . process. It leaves no room for—for the natural way of things. Or for love."

"Nature has been corrupted by men. The world outside has proven that over and over. As for *love*, what exactly do you think it is?"

"Feeling for another as you do for yourself. Love is . . ." Nora glances down at Jude, who lies still on the concrete.

No, he can't be . . .

"Love is the foundation of everything at the Convent," Lilith says. "Our goal is love. Our method is love. You know that."

"Yes, but . . . what I feel for him is different, powerful."

"That is the lie of hormones. It is not truth. It is not reason. We have worked hard to eliminate it."

"But I felt it. I . . . *wanted* it."

"I understand, Nora. That is how the evil contamination works. We have all felt traces of that, but less and less with each genetic selection. Look." Lilith points to the screen. "Your very being soars with talent and yet allows little passion. This is the secret to joy. You will have love here, Nora. You will have the best humanity can hope for."

Nora's soul screams. If there is a lie, if there is evil, it is all that Lilith has said. They have tried to distort Nora from birth, but at her core she knows the truth. What's true is who she was with the boy, the last boy, Jude. What they shared is real. More real than any of this. And that's why she knows she has to put an end to the lies.

"No," she says.

"No?" Lilith's brow lifts in surprise.

"This is not humanity's best. It's only half of humanity. Look at everything around us. The animals, the birds, the flowers. The entire natural order is divided in two. Male and female. Both halves are necessary for the whole."

"They *were* necessary. We have overcome that."

"It's not something to *overcome*. We become our best only alongside males. No one has ever made me feel the way Jude does. No one has challenged me the way he does. You say that I soar with talent, but I've grown more with him than I ever could without him."

"You are young," Lilith sighs. "This *feeling* comes at too great a cost. It is not worth war and destruction and all the evils that testosterone has wrought."

"You're wrong. Testosterone gives them drive and energy and courage. All humanity needs that." Nora remembers Jude's words. "One good man can save the world."

"No," Lilith snaps. "There are no good men."

Nora shudders. She once said the same thing to Jude, and now she's knows it's wrong. "When I was in trouble, Jude would do anything for me. He risked his own life. Call it wild. Call it reckless. It was also love. He would die for me."

"Would he kill hundreds for you? Would he start a war for you? Other men have."

"Not every woman is perfect, either. Would we eliminate apples from the earth because of a few bad ones?"

"Apples we can control. Men cannot be controlled unless we remove their T or medicate them. Now we can dispense with even that risk."

"Only if you stay in this bubble, supported by the Capital, whatever it is. This is not the real world. It won't last. It ends now." Nora grips the gun tighter. "Step away from the computer."

"I see." Lilith holds up her hands. She moves very slowly, cautiously.

"Go to the door," Nora demands.

Lilith nods and moves to pass Nora. As she does, she suddenly swings at Nora.

All Nora sees is a flash of metal. Instinct jerks her arms up, blocking the blow. But the gun is knocked loose from her grip.

Lilith lunges forward. Nora staggers back and presses against a screen. A sharp point is at her throat. Lilith's face moves to within inches of hers.

"Once the evil contaminates," Lilith says, "the only choice is to remove it completely. It saddens me. But I do it for love. We must always put the Convent first, before ourselves and our passions. Goodbye, Nora."

49

♂

Revenge

NO.

Jude dreams the word. It's Nora's voice.

No?

This voice is colder. Crueler.

Not a dream, his shoulder screams. Pain courses through him like electricity, jolting him back into awareness. Something heavy lays over him and pins him down.

Two women are talking. Nora and Lilith. There was a gunshot, right at him. Esau jumped in front. The bullet must have passed through. Hit them both.

His eyes open. Esau's face is before him, pale and lifeless.

I done it for you, Esau said.

". . . I do it for love . . ."

The coldness of the voice lifts Jude's gaze from death to life. Lilith stands close, with a blade at Nora's throat. Her back is to Jude. The muscles in her arm tense. "Goodbye,

Nora."

A feeling of desperation, of love, propels Jude upward. The heavy cabinet slides off him. He crouches, then he leaps. He hits the older woman with all he has.

They're both down. Wrestling.

His right arm is useless, the pain in his shoulder too much.

She gets the upper hand. A slice burns across his thigh.

She raises a bloody blade over him and snarls, "Enough, *boy*."

Nora hits Lilith hard, knocking her off. All three of them scramble. Lilith still clutches the knife. She swings and Nora pulls back. She raises the blade over Jude and stabs down. His arms jerk up and block the blow. A slice opens in his forearm. Blood drips onto his face.

Lilith quickly raises the blade again.

BANG.

A gunshot shatters the air.

A hole appears in Lilith's head. Her face freezes in anger. Her mouth gapes open, but no words come out. The knife clatters to the ground and she falls.

Jude turns away.

Ma is there. Gun in her hand. Tears in her eyes.

"Jude, Jude." Nora clasps his face, leans over him. "You're going to be okay, Jude."

Her face is a halo above him. "Nora."

"Lay still," she says. "I'll get help."

Bright lights gleam down like rays from heaven above. He can't bear it. All goes dark again.

50

♀

Restoration

NORA QUICKLY SCANS THE ROOM. Two mothers, Lilith and Eve, are dead. So is Jude's brother. Only he and his Ma survive, but they're down and bleeding badly. Jude is unconscious but Ma's eyes are open.

Nora rushes to her. "I'll go get help."

"No." Ma's voice is faint. Her hands cover a bloody spot at her side, just below her ribs. "No one can know. By the door . . . there's a medical kit."

"Okay, I'll get it." Nora races to the room's entrance. She opens a box there and finds sutures and compresses and ointments inside.

She hurries back to Ma and sets the box beside her, close to Jude. "What should I do?"

Ma kneels and rifles through the contents. First she pulls out a syringe. She leans over Jude and injects something in his shoulder. Then she injects it into her own side, wincing.

"What does it do?" Nora asks.

"Numbs the pain." Ma takes a needle and thread from the box. "Need to sew it up."

"I'm sorry. I don't know how."

Ma grimaces. "You hold the gauze. Soak up the blood."

Nora swallows. "Okay."

Ma sets to work. With confident and precise movements, she sews up the gaping wound on Jude's wrist. Then she takes tweezers and digs out a bullet from his shoulder and sews up the spot. White bandages go dark red. Finally, Nora watches in amazement as the woman sews up her own wound. The whole operation took only a few minutes.

"That'll do." Ma's face is pale as ice. "We'll be okay, with rest."

"What should I do now?" Nora asks.

"This was recorded. Erase it."

"How?"

"Use the control system." Ma looks to the screens.

"Okay." Nora goes to the place where Eve and Lilith had inputted commands. She gazes up at the screens, which show that the fire has been quelled. Ma is right. No one in the Convent can know what happened here. She finds the screen showing the room she's in. She uses the dashboard to navigate through a series of controls until she finds it. She erases the recording.

No one can know.

"Convent," a man's voice booms from above.

Nora freezes. She looks around and sees no one. She catches Ma's eyes. The wounded woman nods and mouths,

Talk. Calmly.

"Convent, this is the Capital. Do you read me?"

"Yes," Nora says.

"We received your call. What is your report?"

"There was a fire," Nora says. "It's under control now."

"Do you need assistance with the damage?"

"What could you provide?"

"Munitions, medications. It might take us a few hours to get a chopper there. The Cloister had an emergency."

Chopper? Cloister?

A question slips out of Nora. "What kind of emergency?"

"One of them nearly escaped. What about your last boy? Is the situation under control?"

Nora glances to Jude on the floor, his chest rising and falling steadily. Esau lies lifeless beside him. She tries to calm her spinning mind. Ma catches her attention. The woman shakes her head vigorously. She mouths, *It's under control.*

"Yes, it is under control," Nora says. "We're okay without assistance."

"10-4. Your report is overdue."

"We will send it soon."

"10-4. Capital, out."

Nora stares at the speaker that brought the voice. The mothers kept all this secret. Everything she knew was a lie. The truth was hidden beneath her home all these years.

"The Capital will come," says Ma.

Nora turns to her, the woman who was once a mother. "You knew about this."

"Yes. And it's why I left the Convent."

"We have to get you and Jude help."

Ma presses her eyes tight. "My Esau, my John, they're gone."

"I'm sorry. We have to protect Jude now."

Ma meets Nora's gaze again. "We will. You will. You're the lead mother now."

"Me? How?"

"Take Lilith's ruby. Go to her office." Ma's voice rattles, faint and weak. "Call the mothers, one at a time. Tell them the Capital gave you control."

"Won't they resist?"

"Some might, but Lilith is gone. They will obey. They have been taught to do whatever the Capital says."

"What *is* the Capital?"

"It's the government headquarters. They guard our lands and oversee the experiments."

"Genetic experiments?"

Ma nods, pushing herself to her feet. "That's why they created the Convent."

Created. The word hurts. "But . . . *Mother God* . . ."

"The Capital created her, too."

"And the Cloister?"

"We don't know much about it," Ma says. "It's another place like the Convent, a competitor. Long ago, before my time, the mothers traded them boys for jewels. They put males in charge but use similar techniques for reproduction. The Capital controls both places."

Nora presses her hands to her temples. "So it's all a lie?"

"No." Ma's voice is gentle as a sunrise. "This is the life we have been given. We must make the best of it. With you in charge, the Convent can become a fine place. You can learn more about what the Capital is doing. This is an opportunity unlike anything the Convent has ever had. You must be brave."

Nora gazes down at Jude. She remembers the way he charged into the bees, the way he leapt with her off a waterfall. Slowly but fully, a smile spreads over her face. She doesn't need to run away with him and leave the Convent to collapse. She can't abandon the other women. She can give them something they've long needed.

"Yes," Nora says. "I will start by changing things here."

"How?" Ma asks.

Nora answers with the confidence of a mother. "Boys."

51

♂

Future

JUDE PACKS HIS THINGS in his sire's room. He stuffs in a change of clothes, a few jars of food, and a book. It should be enough for a few days. He has survived on far less. He goes to the open window overlooking the waterfall and marvels that he ever had the guts to jump from so high, with a girl no less. They could have died right then and there. They could have been caught. He's sure glad he risked it.

He turns away. He thinks of his brother as he passes the leather chair. If he ever has a son, he figures he'll name him Esau.

He picks up his new fiddle in its case and leaves through the open door. At the end of the hallway, he stops outside the lead mother's office.

"I know, I know," Nora is saying.

"Look, we all appreciate what you're doing," a woman says. "But it's a lot at once. Are you sure we can allow this?"

"It's time for a boy to be born. Valkyrie will do well. She's the toughest woman I've ever known. If anyone can carry and raise a boy, it's her."

"And you're really going to let that . . . sire . . . help?"

"He's the father. He's been here longer than any others. Does anyone doubt his loyalty to the Convent?"

"No, but, I mean."

"It will be okay, Min. This is stage two of a project we've been striving toward for many years. As strange it feels, it is an honor to be part of it."

"Yes, mother."

Jude smiles as he listens. When Nora announced to the surviving mothers that the Capital had selected her as lead mother, she chose Valkyrie and Min as mothers to take the places of Eve and Selene. Selene was given the honor of retirement as a matriarch, responsible for the chicken coop, under Ma's supervision. It has worked better than they hoped. The news of Lilith's death, at the hand of an escaping sire who was also killed, struck so much fear into the surviving mothers that they accepted Nora's report. The mothers know they must obey the Capital in all things. They know the Capital is the source of their energy, their security, their peace.

Jude knocks. The office door opens.

The young woman, Min, stands there in a white robe. She looks uneasy, as if the sight of a boy is still too much to handle.

"Mornin', Min," Jude says.

"Good morning, Jude." She bows and motions for him to enter. "The lead mother is ready for you. All is arranged."

Jude sweeps past her and smiles as he sees Nora. She doesn't look so bad in a white robe, with her short pixie hair and amber eyes, brighter than the ruby at her neck. He holds out his hand. "Shall we?"

She eyes him up and down. "You look better. How's your shoulder doing today?"

"Better than ever."

"Excellent. Min, you will manage things while we're away?"

"Yes, mother."

"And if the Capital calls?"

"You are out hunting for wild boys."

"Indeed." Nora slings her bag over shoulder and takes Jude's hand. "You won't catch half as many as I do."

They walk together from the office and down the hallway and out of the Great Hall. Women stop and gaze at them in wonder as they pass. It's not the first time they've walked together, but it amuses Jude how strange the Convent finds it. A boy walking beside a girl, instead of behind her. A wild boy with a few whiskers, no less.

They will learn true history soon enough, Jude thinks. He credits Nora for thinking of the idea. They are leaving to retrieve the books that are hidden beneath his family's burned home. Jude laughs inside as he thinks of the women in the Convent reading *Paradise Lost.*

Jude holds his head high as he leaves the Convent with his fiddle and a real live girl. Nora leads the way past the red barn, across the familiar field, and along the river into the wilderness.

The sun beams high in the bright blue sky when they reach the Convent's inner fence along the ridge. Nora opens the gate and slips through.

Jude follows her and glances left and right along the gleaming barbed wire. "Think we should tear this fence down?"

"It's the Capital's," Nora says.

"Why would they care? Everything is under control."

"For now." Nora gazes south, where they've learned the Capital is. "I sent Lilith's report to buy us more time. It was dreadful. She wrote proudly of all her successes as a mother. Not a single boy born. Not a single trespasser uncaptured. The only detail she glossed over was a cabin with an exiled couple."

"Ma and Pa."

"Your Ma was Lilith's last connection with sanity."

Jude looks toward the Convent, thinking of Ma as he remembers her in their home, cooking, singing, laughing, and cocking her shotgun. "How are the other women taking to her return?"

"Selene hates it," Nora says. "But most of them are glad to have her back. They were like sisters to her."

"I wish she'd do more than oversee the chicken coop and teach children music."

"It's what she wanted." Nora smiles down at Jude's fiddle case. "And judging by you, she's the best teacher there is."

"Nah," Jude shrugs. "The Convent stifled you, and still,

you're like a whirlwind on stage."

"Good enough to hook you, anyway."

"No question. You caught me."

"I'm pretty sure you're the one who caught me. Kidnapped, actually."

"Yeah, sorry about that." Jude gently touches the side of Nora's head. "Forgive me?"

Nora puts her hand over his. "Yes, now that I've warmed up. You're not so bad, for a boy."

Her amber eyes draw him in. He remembers when steam curled up from her shoulders. "You know," he says, "our hot spring is not too far from here."

She smiles with the innocence of earth's first woman. "Will you play *Primavera* for me again?"

"Your wish is my command."

"Then let's go. I'd love to revisit Eden."

**End of Book One
The Genome Trilogy
♂ ♀**

Acknowledgments

This book is dedicated to my own Ma and Pa. Thanks Mom and thanks Dad for all the homespun tales of life deep in the mountain hollers. Some stories are too good to invent, like when a turtle clamps down on your hand and your mother punches it off. That's tough love. That's strong roots.

I also want to thank the incredible editing team that made this book shine, while I admit that any flaws are mine. As ever, Lindsay, thank you for not letting me settle for anything less than my best (maybe I'll get there in the afterlife). There are too many others to name who helped inspire and polish this story, including Ryan, Daniel S., David, Hannah, Daniel T., Alison, Mindy, Roy, Jens, April, and the rest of the Last Boy advance readers group. Y'all are like rocket fuel for a writer.

And to my kiddos, I'm grateful for you in ways beyond words. But here's a snippet: one day, as I listened to your amazing violin recital, a girl took the stage like a whirlwind and planted the seed for this book. So the story wouldn't exist without you, or Dr. Suzuki. Remember: practice only on the days that you eat.